Old Fashioned Murder

An Arrow Investigations Mystery

KC Walker

Acknowledgements

My stunning cover was designed by Mariah Sinclair. You can find her at https://www.thecovervault.com.

Thank you to Alyssa Lynn Palmer for your copy-editing expertise.

Special thanks to the 1667 Club for the sprints, the laughs, the plot parties, and the fun. You guys mean the world to me.

Finally, most of all to my readers. You give me inspiration, ideas, moral support, and encouragement—and find the most persistent of typos! You are what makes all the hard work worthwhile.

Dedication

To Linda – aka Ukulele Granny

Thank you for all your support through the years. I'm grateful you shared your adventures performing with the Ukulele Grannies. This book would have been very different if it weren't for you.

Keep playing and singing!

Chapter One

The mountain village of Arrow Springs offered activities for the whole family, according to the Arrow Springs Visitor Bureau's brochure. "Enjoy the slow-paced, tranquil lifestyle while you visit our art galleries, unique shops, and world class dining," it read.

Translation: boring.

Small town life suited my seventy-something grandmother, but I was still in my twenties—at least for another few months. The minute the studios called, I'd head straight back to Los Angeles and my job as a stuntwoman. In the meantime, I could do worse than kicking back in one of my grandmother's patio chairs nestled on a pile of sofa cushions.

I'd been staying at my parents' beach house, one of three homes they owned, but that free ride came to an end when my mother gave me an ultimatum: Come stay in Arrow Springs and keep an eye on my grandmother or find somewhere else to live. Considering the state of my bank account, I had few other options, but having the coolest grandmother in town made the decision easier.

It had been seven months since The Incident, as I called it. Surely, another scandal had erupted to give my former coworkers something to talk about besides how I'd flipped a director on his back. After all, he'd deserved it. Instinct had taken over when he grabbed my butt, and if I'd been less impulsive, I might have done something different. A slap across his smug face, perhaps? The thought made me smile.

Closing my eyes, I pondered lunch options, but the forest noises distracted me. Leaves rustled in the wind, birds squawked and twittered, and unknown creatures made scurrying sounds in the underbrush. I liked my wildlife where it belonged: at the zoo where I could keep an eye on it. Even small critters could be deadly, which I learned as a child when my hamster bit my finger and refused to let go.

Behind me, the sliding glass door opened with a squeak, and I glanced over my shoulder, hoping my grandmother had arrived with a muffin or other breakfast pastry to tide me over until our next meal.

"What are you doing out here, Whitley?" she asked in a scolding tone. "It's freezing. I started a fire inside."

I'd snatched an afghan off the sofa, and my favorite combat boots kept my feet warm. At that moment, I regretted cutting all my overprocessed dyed-blonde hair off, but I liked my natural dark brown hair. Besides, my ears would thaw out eventually. "I like the fresh air. I might as well clean out my lungs before I go back to L.A."

"You're not moving back in with Kyle, are you?" She hovered in the doorway, disapproval written all over her face.

"Are you kidding? No way." Kyle had woken up one morning, decided he wasn't in love with me after all, and gave me until the end of the day to move out. I'd be an idiot to take him back, although I wouldn't mind if he begged a little. I'd turn him down gently, of course. Or not.

Kit, the undersized rescue chihuahua my mother had saddled me with, slipped between my grandmother's feet and leapt up onto the deck railing. She walked on the narrow ledge like a pro on the balance beam, much the way I did when I'd been a teenage gymnast.

"Don't let Kit do that," she said, an anxious tone in her voice.

"She's fine, Bobbie." Everyone, including me, called my grandmother Bobbie, with one exception. My mother called her Roberta, which, to be fair, was her name.

Bobbie had an ulterior motive for returning to Arrow Springs. She wanted to get started on her plans to become a private detective, an unusual goal for someone her age. In the past, she'd talked about starting a pottery business, traveling the country in an R.V., and even turning her house into a bed and breakfast. I figured she'd give up on the whole PI thing too when she realized how much work it would involve. Not that she was lazy—on the contrary, she could do anything she put her mind to, but her interest tended to wane once the newness wore off.

Kit's ears rotated like satellite dishes as she scanned for small rodents or lizards, her gaze focused intently on the forest ground from her perch.

"That dog's going to get eaten by a coyote if you're not careful," Bobbie warned.

"Are there coyotes up here?" I asked. "I thought the mountain lions would have chased them off."

Bobbie sighed dramatically and stepped onto the deck to retrieve her. Before she reached the railing, Kit jumped down to the patio, slipped through the slats, and jumped to the ground, running after whatever prey she had been stalking.

Bobbie turned to me, frantic. "Go after her!"

I'd grown attached to the little mutt, so I jumped from my chair and reached the railing in two strides. After a quick assessment of the six-foot drop, I climbed over the railing. She must have jumped onto a pile of wood stacked below on her way to the forest floor, but I decided to jump instead. To avoid breaking any bones, I did a dive roll, which entailed leaping onto a pile of dirt and pine needles and immediately transitioning into a somersault. I sprang to my feet and took off after Kit.

That dog was fast, darting around trees, jumping over branches, and ducking under fallen logs on her way down the hillside. I could have run faster, but with all the rocks and branches, I might have twisted an ankle or worse. For a stuntperson, an injury could be a career killer.

The street lay ahead, and I prayed there weren't any cars about to come around the corner. Kit ran alongside the road, passing a few houses until she stopped and cocked her head as if she'd heard something.

I'd nearly caught up with her when I heard a voice. Or was it my imagination?

"Help!" It sounded faint but not too far away.

Without warning, Kit darted across the road. I panicked and chased after her just as a car came around the corner, tires squealing.

"Slow down!" I yelled at the driver, adding a few choice words as I reached the other side. Kit made a beeline toward an old-fashioned clapboard cottage, disappearing around the back.

"Come back here, you demon," I called out to her.

My feet crunched on the pine needle-covered path which led to the backyard where I found Kit. She wasn't alone. She wagged her tail as she licked the face of a woman lying at the bottom of the steps next to a broken flowerpot. The woman, dressed in a neatly ironed cotton housedress and slippers, didn't seem to be enjoying the tongue bath.

"Gracias a Dios," she said. "¿Puedes sacarme a tu perro, por favor?"

"Huh?" I'd gotten used to people speaking to me in Spanish because of my brown complexion and dark hair, but I had no idea what she'd said. "Habla ingles?"

She gave me a weak smile. "Do you think you could get your dog to stop licking me? And then call an ambulance?"

When I hung up from the call, I crouched next to her. "I'm Whitley Leland. Where are you hurt?"

"Everywhere," she said, clutching her left hand. She struggled to sit up, but I insisted she stay put.

"Keep still until the paramedics arrive. Can I get you a pillow or something?"

She closed her eyes and slowly reopened them. "My head hurts."

"You may have a concussion." In my line of work, I'd had one or two myself. "And your wrist isn't looking good. It might be broken."

Her eyes widened. "Oh my, I hope not. That won't be good at all."

"Is it all right if I go inside your house?" I got another nod in response.

On the way up the steps, I sidestepped an oily puddle. I hurried through the mudroom into the kitchen and retrieved a bag of peas from her freezer, along with pillows and a throw blanket from the living room. On my way back down the steps, I reluctantly swiped my finger along the oily surface and took a sniff. It smelled like baby oil.

She stared at me as I slipped a pillow under her head. "Who did you say you are?"

"Whitley Leland." Lifting her arm gingerly, I slid the other pillow under it to keep it raised. I placed the frozen peas gently on her wrist and wrapped the blanket around her.

"Why does your name sound familiar?" she asked.

"I'm staying with my grandmother, Bobbie Leland. Do you know her?"

"Of course." Her mood improved on hearing my grandmother's name. "You're the acrobat."

"Gymnast. That is, I was a gymnast. When I was a kid, I used to come stay during the summer and train at the Universal Gymnastics Center. I'm a stuntperson now—I just finished up a long-running series and I'm taking some time off until my next job. Everyone calls me Whit."

"I'm Rosa. I taught third grade at the local school until

I retired last year." She looked down at the dog, who'd curled up at her feet. "And who's this?"

"That's Kit," I said. "She's staying with us for a while."

"Hello, Kit." At the sound of her name, Kit's ears perked up. "You're a hero." The dog came closer for some ear scratches. "Who knows how long I would have lain here until someone found me?" She shook her head slowly. "I'm so embarrassed. I've never fallen like that. I'm always so careful. At my age, you have to be."

"You must have slipped on the oil," I suggested.

"Oil?" Rosa's gaze focused on the broken flowerpot. "Oh, dear. My geraniums. I don't suppose they'll pull through this winter." Her eyebrows drew together in confusion. "Did you say oil?"

"It's all over the second step. Baby oil."

"Why would there be oil on my steps?"

I shrugged. "Maybe you spilled some."

Rosa's brow wrinkled in concentration. "What would I be doing with baby oil in the backyard? There hasn't been a baby in the house for a very long time."

A siren wailed, getting louder as it came nearer, and Rosa smiled, probably relieved to have trained medical help on the way. Along with the ambulance came curious neighbors who surrounded Rosa, asking questions and pushing me out of the way.

I stayed until they put Rosa on a gurney, then tucked Kit under my arm like a football and headed home.

Chapter Two

"Where have you two been galivanting about?" Bobbie asked as I returned to my pile of cushions. "I was worried about you. I heard a siren."

"They took your neighbor Rosa to the hospital." I put Kit down and plopped back in my chair.

"Rosa! What happened?" Bobbie looked from me to Kit as if one of us must be to blame.

Before I could answer, I heard pounding. "Is someone at your front door?"

Bobbie leaned over the railing and called out, "Martha? Is that you?"

A woman in gray sweats and pink fluffy slippers came scampering along the side path. She looked to be around my grandmother's age with thin, caramel-colored hair that floated around her head like untamed cotton candy.

"Thank goodness you're back in town!" She climbed

the steps and joined us on the deck, taking a seat on one of the Adirondack chairs. "Have you heard about Rosa?"

"Whit was just about to tell me."

Martha looked my way. "I remember you," she said with a warm smile. "You were a skinny little thing. Weren't you supposed to go to the Olympics, only something happened, and—"

Bobbie interrupted her. "You must have been in a hurry if you rushed out of the house without your shoes."

Martha looked down at her feet and gave an embarrassed laugh. "I didn't even notice!"

Bobbie leaned forward and patted her on the knee. "Is everything all right?"

"Of course," Martha said, rubbing her hands together to warm them. Her smile disappeared. "I mean, no. It's not. Rosa's in the hospital."

"Yes, we know. Whit found her," Bobbie said.

"Actually, Kit did," I corrected.

"Kit?" Martha looked around as if we were hiding another person under a blanket or in a closet.

"Kit is Whitley's dog," Bobbie explained.

I sighed, not ready to accept the role of dog parent. My mother had dropped off Kit and a bag of dog food one day without asking me first. I took it as a passive-aggressive hint that I needed to grow up and become more responsible.

Kit ran over to Martha and rubbed against her slippers, flopping onto her back. Martha reached down and rubbed Kit's belly. "What a sweetheart."

"Do you want a dog?" I asked.

Bobbie reached over and swatted my arm. "She's just kidding."

"No, I'm not." I'd already asked Bobbie if she wanted to keep Kit when I moved back to L.A., but she didn't want the responsibility either. She liked having the dog around, but only if I was there to take her for walks and feed her. That was fine for now, but what about when I got back to work? As if she knew my thoughts, Kit jumped on my lap and licked my chin.

Bobbie stood, ignoring my comment and addressed Martha. "Come inside where it's warmer and have a cup of tea with us."

I thought the weather was the perfect temperature, just the way I imagined fall would be in a place that had seasons, but I didn't want to miss out on possible baked goods. I picked up my coffee cup and followed them into the house. The fireplace made a cozy scene with two floral overstuffed chairs facing it. The fire hissed and crackled, and I found myself hypnotized by the dancing flames.

Silver-framed photographs cluttered the mantelpiece. Some had been there since I was a kid, but there were a few new ones of my parents and one of me—the type of professional headshot that erased all the personality from a person's face. In the picture, my dark, shoulder-length hair was blow dried into soft waves, a style I found far too high-maintenance. Next to it was a snapshot of me in my gymnastics uniform, smiling with a full mouth of braces. What a dork. Later, I'd find a new spot for the photo, like the trash.

An unfamiliar photograph caught my eye. A laughing woman with high cheekbones like mine held onto a straw hat while strands of hair blew in her face. She smiled, but her eyes looked sad. Or was that just me transferring my emotions onto the image of the woman who gave me up? I thought I'd seen all the pictures of Julia, my birth mother, but this one appeared to have been taken more recently than the others.

Bobbie called from the kitchen. "What's taking you so long?"

I joined them in the kitchen where I found Bobbie filling the kettle. I'd wait until we were alone before I asked her about the picture.

She was in the middle of a conversation with Martha. "What did you hear?"

"About what?" Martha sat at the dinette. "Oh, you mean Rosa. I heard she tripped and fell down her back stairs. Is that what happened? How badly was she hurt?"

"The paramedics think she might have a concussion," I said.

"Oh dear." Martha made sympathetic noises.

"And she hurt her wrist," I added.

"What?" Bobbie asked. "Which one?"

"Don't tell me..." Martha said ominously.

I looked from one woman to the other. "Um, it's the left one."

Bobbie shook her head sadly. "She won't be able to play the ukulele for a while."

"Yeah, that's exactly what I was thinking," I said, but my sarcastic wit went right over their heads.

Bobbie disappeared into the pantry and returned with a plate of homemade brownies.

Reaching for one, I asked, "Where were these hiding?"

Bobbie gave me a none-of-your-business look, one I remembered from my childhood. "Whit, would you finish making the tea, please?"

After stuffing the entire brownie in my mouth, I pulled the teapot and three cups out of the cupboard. The urge came over me to practice the cocktail-making skills I'd recently acquired. To earn a few extra bucks over the summer, I'd worked as a bartender, surprised to learn I had quite a knack for concocting delicious libations. It didn't compare to being a stuntperson, but it beat working retail.

"Are you sure you don't want something stronger than tea?" I asked.

"Do you have any sherry?" Martha asked. She blushed and added, "If you're offering."

Bobbie motioned to the dining room. The china cabinet displayed fine china that hadn't been used since my grandfather passed away five years earlier. I opened the doors to the lower cabinet, pleased to see a complete selection of spirits and liqueurs.

"I could make you an Irish coffee." Somehow that seemed a more appropriate pre-lunch drink than sherry. "Or how about a Bloody Mary?"

"Sherry will do, for now," Bobbie called back from the kitchen.

"Fine," I grumbled. "You don't know what you're missing."

I retrieved the bottle and three cordial glasses and set them on the table as the teakettle began to whistle, summoning me back to the stove. Once the teapot and cups were on the table, I joined the two women. I wasn't normally a morning drinker, but I could make an exception just to be sociable.

Bobbie picked up the sherry bottle and poured three generous servings, offering one to Martha. Martha downed it like it was a shot of tequila and held the glass out for Bobbie to refill.

"My, you are shaken up," Bobbie said. "Who told you about Rosa?"

"Gypsy called me. She ran over when she heard the sirens. I hadn't put in my hearing aids yet, so I didn't realize how close they were. Gypsy said by the time she got there, they were loading Rosa into the ambulance. She said there was a young woman with a little dog, but they left before she could ask them anything."

"That was Kit and me."

"Of course." She sipped the second glass of sherry more slowly, her voice calmer now. "Gypsy said Rosa was found at the bottom of her back steps next to a broken pot of geraniums. Is that true?"

I nodded, taking a sip of sherry. It tasted like drunk raisins.

"I just cut them back every winter and hope for the best," Martha said. "Rosa liked to dig them up and bring them inside."

"I've told her it's silly to go to all that trouble," Bobbie said. "Mine come back good as new in the spring."

"You know how some people are." Martha downed the last of her sherry. "Stuck in their ways."

I wasn't sure why talk about their injured friend had turned into a garden club meeting. "She should have been less careless," I suggested.

Martha looked at me as if she didn't know who I was talking about. "Rosa?" She giggled, possibly a little tipsy from the sherry. "Of course, you meant Rosa. She was never careless or sloppy. Nancy always said she almost felt guilty taking money from her for cleaning her house since it was always spotless."

"Nancy is Rosa's housekeeper," Bobbie explained. "She cleans my house, too."

"Mine, too," Martha said. "She does such a good job, and she's very reasonable. I give her a generous tip and a gift card at Christmas. I tell her every year to buy herself something nice, but she always donates it to the local cat rescue."

"She is devoted to those cats," Bobbie said.

Trying to keep these two on topic was impossible, but I tried anyway. "Maybe the inside of Rosa's home was spotless, but there was baby oil on the back steps. I'm guessing she slipped on it."

"That's odd." Bobbie stared at the teapot, lost in thought.

"Do you think it's ready?" Martha asked.

"What?" Bobbie came back from wherever her mind had wandered. "Oh, the tea." She filled the three cups and passed them around. "Would you get the milk, dear?" she asked me.

As soon as I stood up, Bobbie leaned closer to Martha and spoke in a hushed voice.

"Why would there be oil on her steps? Do you think someone put it there?"

Martha seemed taken aback by this question. "Why

would they do that?" When Bobbie didn't answer, she asked, "Do you think someone wanted to hurt her?"

"I think we have to consider the possibility," Bobbie said.

"Hold on now, ladies," I said, returning to the table. I rarely found myself in the position of being the voice of reason. "It was just an accident."

"There have been a lot of accidents lately," Bobbie said. "Too many. I'm starting to think it's not a coincidence. And then there's Sheila's disappearance."

"What are you talking about?" I asked.

"A little over a month ago, Sheila supposedly went to visit her daughter. She left town suddenly after sending a neighbor a text. No one's heard from her since."

"Was she a friend of yours?" I asked.

"Oh, no. She kept to herself, pretty much."

I sighed. "Rosa slipped on some oil, and you haven't heard from a woman you barely know. It doesn't exactly have the makings of a conspiracy."

"I'm sure you're right," Martha said to me, then turned back to Bobbie. "What are we going to do?"

"About the group?" Bobbie asked.

"We're only a quartet now. Do we want to add another player so soon before the competition?"

I felt out of the loop again. "Wait a sec. Now what are you two talking about?"

The two women looked at me as if they'd just remembered I was there. "I must have told you about the Ukulele Ladies," Bobbie said. "There are five of us. Every year, there's a competition with all the local music groups. The winner opens for the main act at the Winter Festival and Craft Fair."

"Plus, there's a big cash prize," Martha explained. "Five thousand dollars."

"Who's your competition?" I asked. "The Kazoo Kids?"

Martha scoffed. "Our biggest competitors are The Tuba Boys, the Soul Sisters, and the Acapella Fellas."

"Uh-huh." It was hard to make jokes when real life was this wacky.

"There's no time to break in a new member," Bobbie said. "We'll have to forge ahead as a quartet."

"Agreed." Martha sighed. "Too bad, though. Rosa was the best musician in our group."

Bobbie nodded in enthusiastic agreement. "Plus, she kept the rest of us out of trouble."

Martha started to giggle. "That's true." She turned to me, a big grin on her face. "Make sure you have Bobbie's lawyer on speed dial."

I didn't even want to know.

Chapter Three

The three-story brick hospital taunted me with its memories. I pretended to check my makeup in the mirror. I wasn't even wearing makeup. "Why don't I wait in the car?" I suggested.

The last time I'd been to this hospital, I'd been a fifteen-year-old patient. I should have known better than to starve myself, but when your coach suggests you might want to lose some weight, and your mother says you're fat, sometimes you overreact.

"Whit?" Bobbie's voice brought me back to the present. "Are you okay?"

"I hate hospitals," I grumbled.

"Everyone hates hospitals. We go because we want to be a good friend and a good neighbor. If I ever end up in the hospital, I want my friends to visit me."

"I don't plan to be hospitalized anytime soon." I left out the obvious fact that my chosen profession made me more likely to be seriously injured than the general population.

"No one plans it, dear," Bobbie said. She clutched a potted African violet and reached for the door handle. Before opening it, she said, "You don't have to go in if you don't want to. I understand."

The note of pity I heard in between her words was like a shot of caffeine waking me from a trance, and in my mind, I heard my gymnastics coach's words: "Never show fear." He used other choice phrases too, such as, "Only sissy girls cry," and "Do you need your mommy?"

I plastered on a smile. "Let's go."

The doors at the visitors entrance swooshed as we stepped through, and I followed Bobbie to the information counter. A fresh-faced young woman greeted us cheerfully and asked us to sign our names in the visitor's log.

The elevator creaked and moaned on its way to the third floor, a journey that felt like it took twenty minutes. I breathed shallowly through my mouth to avoid inhaling the antiseptic smell. As I followed Bobbie down the hallway, I kept my eyes focused on the polished beige linoleum floor and nearly ran into her when she stopped in front of a doorway.

"Rosa," my grandmother called out as we entered the room. "How are you feeling?"

Rosa's thin arm emerged from her baggy hospital gown as she reached for the bedside table. Once she'd retrieved her glasses and put them on, she broke into a wide smile.

"You came." Rosa reached out to Bobbie with her good arm. "And you brought flowers. How thoughtful!"

Bobbie hurried to her side, putting the plant down on

the bedside table. Leaning over to give her a kiss on the cheek, she said, "Of course I came. I brought my granddaughter."

"Oh, yes. It's lovely to see you again. How's your little dog?"

"Kit? She's fine," I said. "I'm still deciding on her punishment for running off the way she did. More importantly, how are you? You're looking better."

"I'm feeling much better." She held up her bandaged left wrist. "My arm is sore, but thankfully not broken."

"Whit told me you fell down the back steps," Bobbie said.

"So clumsy of me." Rosa's cheeks flushed. "I don't remember much, but I do recall your granddaughter suggesting I may have slipped on some oil. I sweep the back steps regularly, and I hose them down when they're dirty, but I suppose I must have missed a spot."

"You never miss anything," Bobbie said. She dragged a chair from the corner of the room, scraping it along the floor, and took a seat next to Rosa's bed. "I don't believe for a minute that you spilled oil on your steps."

Her eyes widened. "Oh, I'm sure I didn't."

"Then how did it get there?" Bobbie leaned closer. "Do you have any enemies who might want to harm you?"

I shook my head. My grandmother had quite an imagination.

The question delighted Rosa. "You sound like one of those detective shows. Do you think someone put a hit out on me?" Her grin indicated she hoped that was the case.

"Don't be stupid." The three of us turned toward the voice. A middle-aged, doughy-faced man wearing a gray polyester shirt and beige slacks stood just inside the doorway, casting a disapproving stare at Rosa. I could spot cheap polyester from a mile away. It wasn't much of a superpower, but someday I hoped it would come in handy.

I returned his disapproving look. Didn't anyone ever tell him that gray and brown didn't go together?

"Hello, Manny," Rosa said. "You remember Bobbie, don't you? This is Whitley, her granddaughter. She's the girl with the dog I told you about."

Manny turned to me. "You're the one who found my mother on the steps and called the ambulance?" His expression didn't show the gratitude I might have expected.

"That's me," I admitted. "My dog Kit actually found her, but I haven't trained her to use the phone yet."

Manny scowled. I hated wasting a good joke on an unappreciative audience.

Addressing Bobbie, Manny said, "Maybe you can talk some sense into her. She's had a very attractive offer on her house. Very attractive," he repeated, I assumed for emphasis. "The Golden Years Retirement Resort has every amenity you could want. Three gourmet meals a day, a gym, and a hot tub. I wouldn't mind moving there myself." He chuckled, but no one laughed with him. His smile evaporated. "I'd feel much better if she didn't live alone."

"That so-called resort is a prison," Rosa said. "They lock the doors, and you can't leave unless you have permission."

"No, Mom, that's just for certain patients with memory impairment."

"Hmph."

He turned back to Bobbie. "I've asked her to move in with my wife and I, but she refuses." When he didn't get a reaction from her, he tried his mother again. "You know Amber and I would love to have you."

"You might, but Amber would make my life miserable. Your wife hates me, and you know it."

"She doesn't hate you, Mom." He sighed dramatically.

Rosa crossed her arms. "I'm staying in my home until they carry me out."

"If you don't want to live with us, I wish you would give Golden Years a chance." He spoke to Bobbie again, possibly hoping for an ally. "They do all the cooking and cleaning, and they have lots of activities."

"Who made the offer on the house?" Bobbie asked.

Manny looked disappointed that Bobbie wasn't helping talk Rosa into moving. "A developer. He's interested in several properties in the area, from what I understand. Are you thinking of selling?" he asked. "Maybe you could both move to Golden Years. Wouldn't that be nice, Mom?" When Rosa didn't respond, he dug a bent card out of his pocket and handed it to Bobbie. She glanced at it before putting it in her purse.

"We should let you get some rest." Bobbie took Rosa's hand in hers and gave it a little squeeze. "I'll come back tomorrow."

"I'm going home later today," Rosa said. "Come by the house tomorrow afternoon for tea. Both of you."

As we made our way back through the hospital halls, Bobbie said, "Me. In a retirement home. Can you imagine?"

I nodded noncommittally. "I don't see what's so bad

with other people doing your cooking and cleaning." I'd grown up in a home where other people did all the menial tasks, and it came as quite a shock when I got my first apartment and had to clean up after myself. Not that cooking was menial—it was an art. Or magic, possibly. I'd never mastered anything more exotic than scrambled eggs. "I wonder how the food is there."

Bobbie wasn't listening to me. "I don't think it was an accident."

"What are you talking about?" I was starting to think she watched too many cop shows on TV. She saw nefarious plots everywhere, which might have explained why she'd signed up for PI classes.

"Last week, Rosa told me someone moved her firewood, and she almost tripped going to her shed. She's not careless, and she's not going senile, before you suggest it."

"I wasn't going to suggest any such thing." Of course, that's exactly what I'd been about to say. Old people did get more forgetful as they aged, but I decided not to point out that fact to Bobbie. Just because her mind was in full working order didn't mean her friend's was. "What's this all about? Don't tell me you were serious when you said you wanted to be a private investigator."

"I suppose you think I'm too old?"

"No."

Of course, she was too old. She was in her seventies, somewhat late in life to start a new career. "Don't you need a law enforcement background to get a license?"

"There are ways to get around it," she said. "I've been doing some research."

We stepped into the bright sunlight. I stopped and

folded my arms. "What is with this family? You all think you can buy your way around any problem that steps in your way. First, my mother bribes the rescue organization to let her have Kit no questions asked—"

Bobbie held up a hand. "I hate to interrupt your rant when you've got such a good head of steam, but I'm not planning to buy my way around the rules."

"Oh." Now I felt sheepish for suggesting it.

"I signed up for online classes, and if I do well, they will help arrange an apprenticeship."

"Really?" I wanted to add "at your age?" but I held my tongue. Once we were in the car, I said, "Tell you what. I'll take you on a stakeout one night, and we can drink coffee out of a thermos and pee in a bottle."

"I don't need a bottle," she said smugly. "I'll just wear a pair of Depends."

I rolled my eyes, wondering what had happened to my sweet old gran who used to be happy knitting and baking cupcakes. I really liked cupcakes.

"When we get home, how about we do some baking?"

She stared out the car window as if watching for something or someone. "You mean, I bake, and you eat."

"I'll clean up." There wasn't much I wouldn't do for cupcakes.

"You mean, you'll lick the bowl."

"That too." That was the best part, after all.

I reached for the gearshift, but before I could put it in reverse, Bobbie placed a hand on my arm.

"Wait," she whispered.

"Wait for what?" I asked. She was staring at the hospital as if it were about to do something suspicious.

All I wanted to do was go home and hopefully eat cupcakes.

She turned back to me, still whispering. "I want to question Manny."

"What are you talking about?" I reluctantly put the thought of baked goods out of my mind for the time being. "And why are you whispering?"

Bobbie kept her eyes on the hospital doors. "There he is," she said as Manny emerged. She opened her door and dashed after him as quickly as her sensible shoes would allow.

By the time I unbuckled my seat belt and chased after her, she was already accosting him.

"Manny," she called out, huffing and puffing.

Manny gave her a cross look but kept walking. He held out his car keys, and an alarm chirped. He eyed us, possibly deciding whether to jump into his car and drive away.

Bobbie stopped to catch her breath. "Do you have a moment?"

"No, I'm sorry. I really don't. I'm late for a meeting."

"Where were you last night?" Bobbie asked. "I think someone put oil on Rosa's back steps hoping she would slip and fall. She's lucky she wasn't hurt worse than she was."

His eyes narrowed. "I don't want you upsetting my mother with your ideas about someone being out to get her."

I joined in, hoping there was still a chance to stay on his good side. "I'm sure that's not what my grandmother means."

Bobbie gave me a scolding look. "That's exactly what I mean. I think someone knew that she comes out early in the morning to work in her yard. Besides, he hasn't answered my question."

"It's none of your business, but if you must know, I was at home with my wife." He got in his car and slammed the door before Bobbie could ask him anything else. Before he drove off, he rolled down his window. "Are you the one who talked her out of moving into a retirement home?"

Bobbie shrugged. "I don't need to talk her out of it. She doesn't want to go."

His face reddened, and he shook a finger at her. "Just stay out of it. I'm only thinking of what's best for my mother." He rolled his window up and backed out of the space.

I had the feeling Manny had some anger issues.

As he drove away, Bobbie muttered, "Everyone knows he sleeps on the sofa."

"Now you're just being catty." Although, if he and his wife weren't on good terms, that might explain why she let him out of the house dressed that way.

"No, I'm not," Bobbie insisted. "Well, maybe a little. But my point is, his wife wouldn't have noticed if he left the house in the middle of the night to go pour oil on his mother's back steps. He seems eager for her to sell her house."

"Maybe he's just worried about his mom," I said. "She did fall and end up in the hospital, you know."

Bobbie huffed. "There's plenty you don't know about what goes on in this town."

Chapter Four

In the eleven days since Bobbie and I had driven up
to Arrow Springs, I'd run every morning, gone to the
local gym six or seven times for strength training,
and explored some local hiking trails. I'd emailed every
stunt coordinator I'd worked with and some I hadn't,
called former coworkers, at least the ones I got along with,
and contacted members of Stunt Works and Stunts
Unlimited. I had checked every website listing upcoming
movie, TV, and commercial productions.

If I didn't find a way to keep myself busy until I got
back to Los Angeles, I'd go crazy. Even if I booked a stunt
job now, it probably wouldn't shoot until after New Year's.
Sure, Arrow Springs was a lovely place to visit. And when
I made it into my seventies, like Bobbie, I might want to
live here.

"How can you live here?" I asked Bobbie as she joined
me on the deck to enjoy her high carb, high sugar breakfast. "There's nothing to do."

"You could work, you know," she said, as if the thought hadn't already occurred to me.

"I'm doing my best. No one is hiring now. Probably won't until after the holidays."

"Not stunt work. Bartending, like you did at the beach. You were surprisingly good at it."

"I was awesome," I said proudly. "Unfortunately, no one's hiring bartenders, awesome or otherwise, right now."

The town would liven up with the first snowfall when the Angelenos came to gawk at falling flakes and risk their lives sliding down hillsides on plastic trash can lids. But that might not be until February.

"I know someone who needs a bartender," Bobbie said. "It's just one evening. This Friday."

"I'll take it," I said.

"Don't you want the details?"

"Nah, I'll just wing it."

Bobbie explained that Ralph, the owner of the Peak Experience Bar and Grille, needed someone to work his booth at the annual Fossil Fest.

"I'll give him a call." Bobbie went into the house while I stared at my phone screen, frustrated at the lack of response. Eventually I'd get another stunt job. I had to.

Bobbie interrupted my ruminations with the news that the job was mine. I agreed without a second thought.

"Rosa is home from the hospital," she informed me. "Why don't we stop by and see her?"

"Why?"

Bobbie looked at me as if I'd been raised by wolves, but since one of those wolves was her son—my dad—I waited for her answer.

"It's neighborly," she said.

"Aren't you supposed to bring her a casserole?"

"Great idea. We'll stop at the General Store on the way."

"They have casseroles at the General Store?" I asked. "And here I always thought people made them from scratch from canned soup and frozen peas."

"No, but they do have Chunky Monkey ice cream. It's her favorite."

Walking through the front doors of the General Store was like stepping back in time. I hadn't shopped there in more than a decade, and it hadn't changed a bit. It lived up to its name, with a passable selection of groceries, along with various other sundries such as propane, firewood, ammo, and liquor.

Scooter stood behind the front counter, and I gave him a wave. He looked up from his magazine and blushed. He'd worked at the store since he was a teenager back when I spent summers in town, which made him a few years older than me.

Making a beeline to the liquor department, I grabbed an overpriced bottle of cointreau, the one ingredient I lacked to make the perfect sidecar. Since my social life these days consisted of watching TV with my grandmother, I figured we might as well have fancy drinks to go along with Bobbie's true crime and British murder mysteries. I assumed we had lemons at home, but I decided it would be smart to ask.

When I finally found Bobbie, she was talking to a man I didn't recognize, so I went to look for lemons. It took me a while to find the tiny produce section, and by the time I got back, she was talking to a woman.

"Whitley," she called out, waving me over. "You remember Gypsy, don't you?"

Gypsy hadn't changed except for getting older. Her long dyed-black hair was as wild as ever, and her drawn-on eyebrows made her appear perpetually surprised.

I said hello, then asked Bobbie if we were leaving soon. She and Gypsy thought this was quite funny.

"Going to the General Store never takes less than an hour," Bobbie informed me.

"Well, I wouldn't take too much longer, or your ice cream will be chocolate soup."

"Actually, Chunky Monkey is banana flavored. That's where the name comes from."

"Good to know," I said, doing my best to keep the sarcasm out of my voice. "I'll wait for you in the car."

Bobbie took the hint and picked up a copy of the *National Enquirer* to go with the ice cream. Scooter was even taller and skinnier than he was as a teenager. I judged him to be about six foot four and 150 pounds at most. His thick, sandy brown hair looked like he'd cut it himself with garden shears.

He rang us up, and Bobbie even paid for my liqueur. I made a mental note to go shopping with her more often, even if it did take an hour to buy three things.

"Scooter has it bad," Bobbie said as we walked to the car.

"What? He's ill?" He looked pale, but I figured he just didn't get out much.

"Lovesick," she said, snickering. "He's had a crush on you since you spent your summers here."

"Stop it, please. I was like twelve."

"He's not much older than you," she said.

I chose to drop the subject of Scooter and his crush, hoping she'd never, ever mention it again, and drove to Rosa's house.

Five minutes later, Bobbie and I stood on Rosa's porch, Bobbie holding her offerings.

Rosa's son, Manny, opened the door. "Oh, it's you," he said in greeting.

"Did we catch you at a bad time?" Bobbie asked sweetly.

Retreating into the house, he called out, "Mom, you've got visitors."

We took that as an invitation and stepped into the living room. Rosa limped to the kitchen door, one arm in a sling. Her face lit up when she saw us. "Come in, come in. I just made a pot of coffee. Join me."

Handing over the ice cream and the magazine, Bobbie pulled out two upholstered vinyl chairs and sat down at the matching red Formica dining table, gesturing for me to join her.

Bobbie and Rosa caught up on all the local gossip and, thanks to the *Enquirer*, the national gossip as well. I took a couple of sips of the weak coffee and let my mind wander as they chattered on.

I'd nearly drifted to sleep when I heard Bobbie mention my name. "What?"

Bobbie lowered her voice. "I just told Rosa you're going to help me get to the bottom of the accidents." She went on to explain her theory to Rosa. "I think someone wants to win the competition so badly, they're trying to sabotage us."

Rosa's eyes widened. "Trying to sabotage who?"

"The Ukulele Ladies."

Rosa looked from Bobbie to me and back to Bobbie. "But why would they do that? We haven't won once in the last ten years."

Bobbie frowned as she processed Rosa's comment. "You're right. They would have gone after the Soul Sisters. They've won the past three competitions."

"Now that that's settled," I said, "do you have any other brilliant theories?"

Bobbie raised her eyebrows, but I was at a loss as to how to interpret her expression. Then she gestured with a jerk of her head toward the living room.

"Manny?" I asked.

"What?" Rosa asked, startled.

Bobbie rolled her eyes, no doubt disappointed in my lack of mind reading skills.

"Nothing."

"No, I want to know." Rosa lowered her voice to a whisper. "If you think Manny had something to do with my accident, you couldn't be more wrong. He's been taking wonderful care of me."

"He wants to put you in a home," Bobbie said.

Rosa dismissed the idea with a wave of her hand. "He just thinks it would be easier on me if I didn't have a big house to take care of. He wants me to move in with him, but his wife... well, let's just say we don't see eye to eye. Moving to a retirement home like Golden Years wouldn't be so terrible. They provide all your meals at those places, you know."

"You're not actually considering it, are you?" Bobbie made it sound like an accusation.

"Not right now." She pulled her shoulders back and lifted her chin. "But, someday, I might need someone to take care of me."

Rosa and Bobbie must have had this discussion before, and the tension in the room told me they hadn't yet agreed to disagree. A pang in my stomach reminded me that Bobbie had promised me lunch. I tapped her shoulder. "Ready to go?"

Bobbie nodded, then reached over and took Rosa's hand. "Call me if you need anything. Or if you notice anything suspicious."

After thanking Rosa for the coffee, I turned toward the door and saw Manny listening from the living room. The moment I made eye contact with him, he ducked out of sight.

Chapter Five

Friday night, I walked into the living room, tugging at the bottom of a faux-fur cavewoman dress, trying to make sure it covered all the essentials.

"Is that what you're wearing to tend bar at Ralph's booth?" Bobbie asked, trying to keep a straight face.

"Don't pretend you didn't know." I scowled and searched for the fur hat Ralph had sent over, finally retrieving it from Kit, who'd dragged it under the sofa thinking it was her newest chew toy. The hat had a tail with spikes that went down the back to my waist like a furry stegosaurus. Was I supposed to be some sort of mutant cavewoman? "You could have warned me."

She snickered but wouldn't admit guilt. "You're wearing sneakers?"

I sighed and went back in my room to retrieve the fur covers designed to hide my shoes. "I better get some good tips tonight."

"Here's your first," she said. "No matter how thirsty

you get, stay away from the tar pits."

"Very funny. Do you want a ride into town?"

"Sure," she said. "Are we going on the back of your triceratops?"

"Watch out, or I'll get you with one of my spikes." I turned my head quickly swinging the tail of my hat toward her and hitting myself in the face instead. "Or, better yet, I'll make you walk there."

"They're called osteoderms," she corrected me. "Not spikes."

"Good to know." That information might come in handy if I were a Jeopardy contestant, or if I ever dated a paleontologist. I filed it away in my mind with the rest of the random trivia I'd learned from my grandmother.

In the center of town, three streets formed a triangle with a park in the center, complete with a gazebo, picnic tables, and the statue of Franklin Norvelt, the founder of Arrow Springs. Originally, Norvelt had envisioned a utopian community in which members held assets in common. That lasted twenty years, until his death, when the townspeople voted to incorporate to avoid being taken over by Big Springs, a town overrun by tourists most of the year.

Bobbie directed me to the Peak Experience Bar and Grille parking lot, where I told the attendant I was working for Ralph, so I didn't have to pay for parking.

The restaurant, an oversized log cabin, faced the park. Wooden sidewalks led from shop to shop, giving the town an Old West feel. Family activities had started earlier that day, and now people milled about, window shopping and strolling with locally made beef jerky and hot cider. The moment the late afternoon sun dipped below the trees, the temperature would drop at least ten degrees, and I'd want to find my own hot toddy.

I got out of the car and found Ralph around the back of the restaurant, lifting boxes of supplies onto a hand truck. At least I assumed it was him, since we'd only talked over the phone. I hurried over, leaving Bobbie to fend for herself.

"Do you need help with that?" I called out.

Ralph must not have seen or heard us coming, or he startled easily, because he jumped at the sound of my voice. He wasn't bad looking for an old guy, and he appeared to be in great shape, judging by the ease with which he lifted cases of vodka and sour mix.

"Hi, I'm Whitley."

"Nice to finally meet you, Whitley." He gestured to my outfit. "You look great."

"You might have mentioned I'd have to wear a costume before I accepted the job."

"It's all in fun." He chuckled, then his face lit up the moment he saw my grandmother. "Nice to see you." His casual greeting didn't fool me for a second—he had a thing for Bobbie.

"You too," she replied.

Bobbie showed no reaction to his obvious interest. Ralph handed me a bag of supplies and said he'd meet us at the booth shortly.

"You don't make your own sour mix?" I asked. I didn't mean to be judgmental, but the first rule of making a great cocktail was freshly made sour mix.

"Ordinarily, yes," he said, "but not this weekend. This

is the first time I let the committee talk me into putting up a booth. It's a lot of work, and we run a skeleton crew this time of year."

That explained why he'd recruited me to help. "Who's bartending with me tonight?"

"Just you and me until seven, and then I have reinforcements arriving. You can call it a night around eight. I really appreciate you helping me out."

Bobbie and I crossed the street under banners announcing, "17th Annual Fossil Fest." The event had been the brainchild of the late Mayor Mishchuk, the father of the current mayor.

"Ralph seems nice," I said, doing my best to sound nonchalant. "Do you see a lot of each other?"

"Yes, of course," Bobbie said. "He's one of the Ukulele Ladies."

"He's what?"

"I think you heard me," she said, speaking to me in that tone used for small children. "He's an excellent ukulele player, and he has a car, so that's a plus. We offered to change the name of the group, but he insisted he didn't mind."

I reflected on how things always came back around. As a teenager, if a boy had a car, it made him immensely popular, and apparently it was the same when you got to be Bobbie's age.

"And don't go trying to fix us up," she continued. "I get more offers than I want. I loved your grandfather, but fifty years of looking after a man was enough for me. I wouldn't mind the companionship, mind you, but now that they have that little blue pill—"

"Ew, gross," I said, raising a hand. I prayed she wouldn't bring it up again.

In the middle of the park, tables with games and crafts for the youngsters surrounded Norvelt's statue. A middle-aged man sat atop the obligatory dunk tank, and I hoped for his sake that he stayed dry. Unlike most of Southern California, the temperature in the mountains could dip below freezing this time of year.

Booths lined the perimeter of the park, most serving food or drink while others overflowed with souvenirs and dinosaur trinkets, along with hippie paraphernalia, like crystals and candles. New Age shops flourished in Arrow Springs, helped in part by Bobbie's patronage. I stopped to admire a foot-tall chunk of amethyst.

"That would help you clear the negativity in your aura," a male voice said in a soft, soothing tone, like a monk recruiting me into a cult.

I turned around, ready to release my negativity on the speaker. Before me stood a tall, dark-skinned man around my age or perhaps a few years older, smiling at me as if we were old friends. I never thought an organic cotton tunic could look sexy, but he made it look good.

"Well, hello," I said, suddenly self-conscious of my teeny-tiny skirt. "I'm working tonight," I said in explanation, gesturing at my bare legs and instantly regretting it. "At the Peak Experience booth. As a bartender," I added, just in case he thought I was a different kind of working girl.

My grandmother interrupted my awkward flirtation attempt. "Hello, Elijah," she said to the hunk. "I thought you'd be helping out at your mother's booth."

"She decided to give it a pass this year," he said. "The owners of Mystical Treasures asked me to help with their booth, and I thought it might be fun. Do you know them?"

"The sisters? I've met them," Bobbie said. "They're a little spooky, if you ask me."

Elijah chuckled. "You're not the only one who thinks so. They'll be here later doing tarot readings." He turned back to me. "You should stop back by."

"I'll try," I said. "I'm Whit, by the way."

"I know." His smile warmed me on the inside. "Nice to meet you."

Bobbie followed me to Ralph's booth but didn't help carry any supplies. I guessed that was a perk of getting older. The wooden structure had a large painted sign with the restaurant's name and a smaller laminated listing of drink offerings.

I plopped the bags onto the back counter. "Why didn't I know about the handsome man walking around town? Are there more? What other secrets are you keeping from me?"

"Don't be silly," she said. "Why would I keep secrets?" She gazed at the surroundings, avoiding eye contact.

"And why does he know who I am?"

"Elijah is Gypsy's son. But it's like you're new in town since you've spent so little time here since you quit gymnastics. I'm sure by now everyone knows you're back in town."

"I hate small towns," I grumbled. I liked the anonymity of a big city where people didn't know your business.

"You used to love coming here for the summer."

I didn't want to talk about what used to be, so I stuffed my parka in a cubby and began setting up while Bobbie leaned on the counter, people watching.

"As soon as the sun goes down," I said, "I'm putting my jacket on even if it isn't themed for the occasion."

Bobbie wasn't listening. Her attention had been drawn to two older ladies talking. I would have recognized Rosa even without the sling on her arm, but I didn't know the other woman who gestured wildly while Rosa tried to calm her down.

"I'd better see what's up." Bobbie stomped off, so I got started setting up the bar.

I sliced lemons and arranged cocktail umbrellas so they'd be ready when I needed them. Offering hand-shaken cocktails at a fair, even with a limited menu, seemed crazy. When we'd talked on the phone earlier, I'd suggested pre-mixed drinks with cute names like a Dino-tini and Mai Tyrannosaurus Rex. Ralph had chuckled at my suggestions, but he'd already printed out menus.

At least I wouldn't have to handle money, since it was a ticket-only transaction. The booth that sold tickets gave you a wristband if you were over twenty-one, so I wouldn't have to check IDs either.

"Hello, cavewoman," a male voice said. "Or is it cave lady?"

This was going to be a long night. "We're not open until five," I said, not bothering to see who was talking.

"You don't recognize me, do you?"

I looked up, squinting in the floodlight that illumi-nated the front of the booth. I would have remembered such a fine specimen of manhood. Tall with nice muscles showing through his long-sleeved T-shirt, he looked like someone who could literally sweep a woman off her feet. Not quite a ginger, but I would have bet there were freckles somewhere on his body.

"Sorry if that sounded like a bad pickup line." His voice sounded less confident, as if he'd suddenly become shy. "It's me, Luke."

"Luke?" I hadn't been back to Arrow Springs for more than a quick visit since my teens. The only Luke I remembered from my teenage years was a skinny, nerdy kid two years younger than me who had reddish hair and braces. It couldn't be. "Luke, who played the saxophone?"

He smiled, displaying a perfect set of pearly whites. I found myself grinning, wondering how stupid I must look and reminding myself not to drool.

"That's me," he said.

"Wow." I thought about other words I might say. "It's been a long time. What have you been doing all these years?" Getting married and having kids? I wanted to ask but told myself to be patient. I did notice he wasn't wearing a ring.

"I went to USC as a music major and got my master's at Juilliard."

"Uh-huh." I leaned up against the bar, content to watch him as he talked.

"I toured with a jazz band, but that got old after a year." He looked pensive for a moment as if lost in a memory. "So, I came back and got a job teaching here at the Arts Academy. Not as exciting as touring, but I like sleeping in the same place every night." He gave me a knowing look. "Or at least most nights."

Did he mean what I thought he meant? "Um..." I began, trying to remember how to use my words.

"Excuse me," a gruff, male voice said.

"Not now," I replied without thinking, not taking my eyes off Luke.

"Excuse me," the man said louder this time. "I'd like an Old Fashioned."

"We don't open until five," I answered.

"It's five o'clock right now, and I have a ticket."

"Oh, sorry." I gave the man a repentant smile. "I'll be right with you." I turned to say something to Luke, and what came out was, "Do you run?"

"Yeah, I do." Luckily, he got my hint. "Meet you tomorrow morning by the bear? Say seven?"

"Seven it is." I turned to make Mr. Impatient his drink. Darn. I should have asked what he meant by "the bear."

The line for drinks soon stretched out like a brontosaurus tail, and I sighed with relief when Ralph joined me at the booth. If only he'd gone for the pre-mixed cocktails, we would have gotten through the line in no time.

"Psst."

I looked for the source of the sound and saw my grandmother gesturing to me. After handing the cosmopolitan I'd just mixed to the man at the front of the line, I acknowledged Bobbie.

"Hi, what's up? Want me to make you a Whiskeysourus?"

The young woman at the front of the line objected. "Hey, I was here first."

"I don't want a drink," Bobbie said. "I need to talk to you."

"Okay, I should have a break coming up soon." I glanced over at Ralph to see if he got the hint.

"Are you going to talk or make drinks, Wilma Flintstone?" the woman asked.

"Give me a sec, lady," I said.

Ralph nudged me. "Break time!" He turned to the woman. "What can I get you?"

I came out from behind the booth, hoping no one I knew would see me in the tiny skirt. Then I looked around and realized I was neither the oddest nor the sluttiest dressed female in attendance.

"I didn't know they made sexy T-Rex costumes," I commented to Bobbie. "Those little, short arms really don't—"

She interrupted my fashion commentary. "Martha is missing. She was supposed to meet friends for lunch, and she didn't show up."

I sighed. Not this again. "Maybe she wasn't feeling well."

"Rosa and Gypsy went over to Martha's to check on her, and she's not home."

"So, she went out," I suggested, knowing that the answer Bobbie wanted leaned more toward foul play.

"Where?" Bobbie scowled in frustration. "Every place in town is closed this evening. Everyone is here, at the Fossil Fest."

"Then she's probably here, too. It would be easy to get lost in this crowd." When Bobbie shook her head, I did my best to be reassuring. "I can tell you're worried."

"We can talk about our feelings later. Right now, we need to do something."

"Fine," I said. "As soon as I'm done here, we'll go over to Martha's house and check on her."

"What time?"

"Eight o'clock," I said. "In the meantime, why don't you ask around and see if someone's seen her? Maybe she got lucky."

"Got lucky?" Bobbie repeated, eyes wide. "I hope you're suggesting she won the lottery."

"That's exactly what I was suggesting," I fibbed.

The booth got even busier when the sun went down. The families took their rug rats home, and the serious drinking began.

Ralph and I made drink after drink, and at one point he said, "If I do this again next year, we're definitely doing pre-mixed cocktails."

As soon as the relief bartender arrived, Ralph gave me the rest of the night off. Bobbie's nervous pacing while she waited for my shift to end might have influenced his decision.

As we hurried to my car, I mentally thanked my mother for buying me the parka that went down to my knees. I glanced over at Bobbie whose scowl had only deepened as her worry increased.

"I'm sure your friend is fine," I said, trying to reassure her again. I don't know why—that stuff never works on me, and it didn't work on Bobbie.

"You may be sure, but I'm not. I think something terrible has happened."

Chapter Six

I pulled into Martha's driveway, leaving my headlights on so we'd be able to see our way to her front door. There were few streetlights away from the center of town, which made stargazing a real treat for a city girl like me, but going for midnight walks could be hazardous.

The moment I stopped the car, Bobbie opened the door and climbed out. Being younger and faster, I made it to the front door first and gave it three sharp raps. After a short wait, I raised my fist to knock again, but Bobbie pushed me aside and pounded on the door. I glanced up at the sky but couldn't spot a single star. A half moon glowed weakly behind the cloud cover.

Bobbie began rooting around the potted plants on either side of the door. Before I knew it, she produced a key and shoved it into the door lock.

"What are you doing?" I asked.

"You coming?" She pushed open the door and called

out, "Martha? Martha, are you here?" Reaching for the light switch, she flicked it on, then off and on again, but nothing happened. "No power."

After going back to the car to turn off my headlights, I entered the living room, a Smithsonian exhibit for the seventies with dark wood paneling and harvest gold carpet flattened by years of wear. My phone's flashlight illuminated a pair of orange velour recliners facing a flat-screen TV mounted on the wall, the room's one capitulation to modernity.

While Bobbie moved through the house, I stopped to admire a veneer stereo console complete with built-in speakers until she reappeared.

"She's not in her bedroom." When my grandmother took my phone from me, I followed her to the kitchen. She shined the light slowly around the room as if scanning for something out of place. The small, utilitarian kitchen with its white walls and avocado appliances sparkled in the beam. Besides the appliances, the only other touches of color were tiny blue and red flowers embroidered on white café curtains. Clean plates stood neatly in a dish drainer next to the sink, left to dry.

"Are you sure we should be in here?" I asked.

"Of course," Bobbie said. "Look at those dishes. If she went out, why didn't she put them away?"

"You think that's suspicious? I've left dirty dishes in the sink for days, and these are clean. Is there some kind of rule about putting dishes away as soon as you wash them? Aren't you supposed to wait for them to dry?"

Bobbie shook her head, as if ashamed of my lack of knowledge of dishwashing etiquette. I shrugged. I knew my limitations, which was why I stocked up on paper plates.

Reclaiming my phone from Bobbie, I aimed the beam at the dishes and picked up a bowl. "It's chipped. Why doesn't she throw it away?"

"Not everyone throws things away when they get old or worn."

"Whatever." I hoped I wasn't in for another economics lecture meant to make me feel guilty for being born into a wealthy family. What was the point of feeling guilty about something you couldn't change?

It felt weird to be in someone else's house when they weren't home and didn't know you were there. "What if she showed up now?"

"She would be very happy to know I cared enough to make sure she was okay."

Bobbie found a flashlight in one of the drawers and flicked it on. I followed her into the bathroom and leaned on the door jamb while she snooped through the medicine chest.

"What are you looking for?" I asked.

"I'm looking to see if anything is missing." She held a bottle of prescription medication out as far as her arms would allow, attempting to decipher the label. "Heart medication," she said before putting it back. She gestured to one of those daily pill cases labeled with the days of the week. "Notice how Monday through Saturday are empty but the spot for Sunday still has pills in it? That means she hasn't left town."

Just because I'd snooped through a few medicine cabinets in my time didn't mean I wanted to be caught in the act. "I'm going to wait in the kitchen."

Pulling up a chair at the dinette, I sat in the dark and checked my phone for messages. My favorite stunt coordinator had answered one of my emails. She'd been hired to work on a new series and wrote that she might have a job for me.

"Yes!" I might be back in L.A. in no time.

A sharp rap on the door nearly made me jump out of my chair. "Bobbie, someone's at the door."

"Well, answer it then," she called back from the bathroom.

The rapping was louder and more urgent, so I went to the door and peered through the peephole. I couldn't see much in the dark, but I did see a badge on a uniform.

I opened the door, holding my breath. He wasn't pointing a gun at me, so I exhaled. "Hello, may I help you?"

"I'm Deputy Wallenthorp." The officer flashed his credentials. "May I come in?"

"Of course." I stepped back so he could enter. In the dark, it was hard to tell his age. I guessed him to be around fifty. He had an air of rugged strength, but I'd been to enough dimly lit bars to know better than to make assumptions.

He pulled out his flashlight and shined it in my face. My hand jerked up to shield my eyes.

"Hey," I said. "Can you not do that?"

He flicked on the wall switch. "Power's out."

I clamped my mouth tightly to keep from saying something I'd regret, like "Duh." What came out instead was,

"Yes, that's why we're standing in the dark." A hint of sarcasm might have crept into my voice.

"We had a call that Mrs. Randall might be missing," he said, just as Bobbie came out of the back bedroom. He directed his beam at her torso, thoughtfully not blinding her the way he had me. "But it appears you're here and well."

"I am quite well, but I'm not Mrs. Randall."

"Then what are you doing here?"

"We're looking for signs of foul play."

I looked at the officer and shrugged, hoping he had a wacky old lady in his family and wouldn't arrest us for breaking and entering. "She was worried about Martha, so we came to check on her. No one's seen her all day."

"How long since you've heard from her?"

"Not since this morning," Bobbie explained. "She'd made plans for lunch but didn't show. She was also supposed to meet a group of friends at the Fossil Fest. It's not like her to blow them off like that."

The officer dug in his pocket for a card, handing it to Bobbie. "If she doesn't turn up by tomorrow, come down to the station and file a missing person's report."

"She might be dead by then," Bobbie said, her voice rising.

Wallenthorp's eyes widened. "Is she in need of medical attention?"

"No," I said. "She's in great health for her age. Thank you for your help."

I closed the door and turned to Bobbie, who glared at me as if I'd done something wrong. "She might be dead?" I repeated. "You have definitely been watching too many crime shows lately. We're leaving now."

Bobbie sulked but followed me to the door. She stopped to take one last look around when we both heard a meow.

"Mr. Whiskers!" Bobbie exclaimed.

"Mr. Who?"

"Martha's cat."

The sound led us to the back of the house and the basement door. Bobbie pulled it open, and a blur of black and white fur flew past us.

"What was the cat doing in the basement?" Bobbie aimed her flashlight down the stairs and took a few tentative steps. She swept the beam across the basement floor until she froze in place. I peered over her shoulder to see what she'd spotted.

A woman lay face down in a puddle of water. With a sinking feeling, my gaze traveled from her caramel-colored hair to the pink fluffy slippers on her feet.

"Wait," I called out as I chased my grandmother down the steps. A frayed wire lay menacingly on the ground touching the puddle. I held out a hand as I stepped clear of the wet area and found the fuse box against the wall. With no power, it probably wasn't a danger, but I wasn't about to take the chance. I opened the cover to cut off the power. Something about the position of the switches seemed odd. I pulled out my phone and took a picture, then flipped all the switches to the off position.

The moment I gave the okay, Bobbie rushed to Martha's side, kneeling beside her on the wet concrete. While she frantically checked for a pulse or other signs of life, I called the paramedics. My gut told me they'd arrive too late to save her, but I hoped otherwise.

When I'd hung up the phone, I crouched next to Bobbie and touched Martha's arm. Her body felt cold. Too cold.

"Help me turn her over," Bobbie pleaded. "I need to perform CPR."

It broke my heart to have to be the one to steal my grandmother's hope. I gently lifted one of Martha's arms, which yielded stiffly. Bobbie watched me wide-eyed and began to sob.

I didn't know a lot about dead bodies, but I knew that rigor mortis meant she'd been gone for a while.

Martha must have gone into the basement to check the fuse box when the lights went out. Somehow a live wire had come loose, falling into the puddle of water and electrifying it. With her bad heart, Martha must have gone instantly.

Bobbie held onto Martha's hand, speaking softly to her as if she could still hear. Meanwhile, I searched for the source of the leak that had caused the basement to flood. Behind the washing machine, one of the hoses had come loose from the faucet. It must have been dripping for hours, a slow dribble of water. What an unlikely combination of events—by themselves, a flooded basement or a loose wire would have been an inconvenience, but together they were deadly.

The paramedics arrived and officially pronounced Martha dead. I coaxed Bobbie out of the basement to wait for Deputy Wallenthorp. We didn't have to wait long.

"I guess your instincts were right, Mrs. Leland," he said.

"I wish they hadn't been," Bobbie mumbled, still overcome with emotion.

"I'm sorry for the loss of your friend. I'll need to ask you some questions, but if you're not up to it now, you can—"

"Let's get it over with." Bobbie blew her nose and took a seat at the kitchen table.

The deputy sat across from her while I stood next to Bobbie, one hand on her shoulder. He asked us a few questions about Martha and told us he'd call if he needed more information. "These sorts of accidents happen from time to time," he mumbled.

Bobbie closed the door behind the deputy. She sniffled and dabbed at her eyes with a tissue. "I'll get Mr. Whiskers so he can come home with us."

"Just put some food out and check the litter box," I suggested. "He deserves better than to be taken to a house with a hyper chihuahua."

Bobbie seemed taken aback by my sensible idea. "Leave him here? Alone? After he's been traumatized by being trapped in the basement with his- his-" She couldn't finish the sentence. She didn't have to.

"Isn't there someone else you can call to take him? Wouldn't he be more traumatized by being in a strange place with a dog?"

"I'm sure they'll get along great," Bobbie said, not able to hide the doubt in her voice. "You'll see. They'll be fast friends in no time."

Chapter Seven

The moment we stepped inside, Kit emerged from wherever she'd been hiding. She ran up to me, bouncing up and down, until Mr. Whiskers gave a soft mew. Turning her attention to Bobbie and the creature in her arms, she froze, her ears coming to attention. A guttural sound began in her throat, increasing in volume to a full-grown growl, and she lowered her head in a less than welcoming gesture.

"It's okay, Kit," Bobbie said in her sweetest tone. "I brought you a new friend." Leaning over, she plopped Mr. Whiskers on the floor before I could stop her.

The cat crouched, low to the floor, and the two animals engaged in a staring contest. Who moved first I couldn't tell. Kit pounced, letting out a loud, sharp bark just as the cat swung a paw, claws bared. Bobbie's yells mixed with the frantic yelps from Kit and a blood-curdling howl from Mr. Whiskers until the two pets ran away—Kit to her perch on the back of the sofa and Mr. Whiskers behind the china cabinet.

"Well, that went well." I managed to refrain from saying, "I told you so."

Bobbie scolded Kit half-heartedly, "That's no way to treat a guest," before heading straight for the refrigerator with me right behind.

She pulled out a bottle of pinot grigio, so I grabbed a couple of glasses. After spending the evening serving hundreds of cocktails and discovering a dead body, I was ready for a drink myself. I didn't say a word until we were settled in the living room with our wine. Eventually, Bobbie coaxed Kit off her perch, and the dog snuggled under the afghan on her lap.

To break the silence, I quietly said, "It must be a huge shock losing your friend like this. Do you want to talk about it?"

Her red-rimmed eyes held mine in a determined gaze. "What I want is to find out who murdered Martha."

It seemed premature to come to that conclusion, but if investigating Martha's death distracted Bobbie from her grief, I didn't see the harm.

"Do you know much about fuses?" I asked. "I looked in the fuse box and one of them was in the off position and another was half-way off. Does that mean she blew two fuses?" Maybe the live wire in the water had done it.

"No one has fuses any more. They're breakers. If one is tripped, you have to turn it all the way to the off position before turning it back on."

"Then I don't get this." I showed her the picture I'd taken of what I now knew was a circuit breaker.

Bobbie's eyes widened and she snatched the phone from me. "Someone turned off one of the breakers. Flipped it manually." She enlarged the photo and pointed to one of the switches. "See, this one is on the off position." She stared at the photo again. "What I don't understand is why the breaker didn't flip when the live wire electrified the puddle. I thought that's what breakers were for."

"Do you know any electricians we can ask?"

Bobbie thought for a moment. "Ralph is pretty handy —he might know. And I'm sure Gypsy knows someone since she just had her restaurant kitchen redone after her fire. I don't know who's engineered all these accidents targeting my friends, but I'm going to find out who did it. I bet it's all connected."

"This is the second time you've mentioned accidents. What's that about?"

"Let's see." She held up one finger. "Besides Rosa's accident, Gypsy had a fire at her restaurant late at night. She managed to stop it from spreading from the kitchen, but ended up with smoke inhalation." Now she had two fingers raised.

"Okay." A kitchen fire wouldn't normally seem suspicious, but I withheld judgement.

"Next," another finger went up, "Vanessa found a poisonous snake in her bathtub."

"Well, that could happen living in the mountains." From now on, I'd check carefully when I pulled the shower curtain back. I'd probably better check the toilet too. Ugh. And people thought cities were dangerous.

"It's never happened to me. Or anyone I know before

now." She gave a shiver, maybe imagining bathtub snakes, too.

"There's always a first time." I'd have to do an internet search for snake repellant.

"And now Martha is dead."

I lifted the wineglass to my lips and took a long sip, my mind racing with possibilities. Anecdotally, that seemed like a lot of accidents for a small town like Arrow Springs, but not outside the realm of possibility. The fact that they were all friends of Bobbie's made it more suspicious.

"When was the first accident?" I asked.

Bobbie gave my question some thought before replying. "Gypsy's fire happened a couple of months ago. I think that was the first." She narrowed her eyes. "Why do you ask?"

"Not sure. Do Gypsy, Rosa, and Vanessa have any connection besides the fact that they're all, shall I say, mature women?"

Bobbie's hand flew to her chest, and I worried she was having a heart attack.

I jumped up from the sofa. "Are you okay? What can I get you?" I grabbed my phone, ready to call the paramedics again.

She reached up to clutch my arm and pull me back down to the sofa. "They're all in the competition. Rosa, Gypsy, and Martha are—were—Ukulele Ladies. Vanessa's a Soul Sister. That must be why they've been targeted."

I blinked, trying to decipher her logic. "That makes no sense. What did you say the prize was? Five thousand? No one would go to those lengths for five thousand dollars. Would they?"

"That's a lot of money for some people."

"But enough to murder someone?"

"Maybe Martha wasn't supposed to die," Bobbie said.

"So, it was just a prank that went wrong? Or a scare tactic?" That didn't sound all that far-fetched. "We need to find out if the voltage from the loose wire would normally be enough to kill someone."

"A rattlesnake bite wouldn't normally be fatal," she said. "As long as you get medical treatment. But it can result in long-term pain or numbness for months or even years." She must have noticed the surprised look on my face because she added, "I looked it up on Wikipedia."

"So, you think someone's going around injuring women to make them drop out of the competition?"

Bobbie barely suppressed a yawn.

"You're tired," I said. "Why don't we sleep on it? We'll talk in the morning."

"I bet I won't get a wink of sleep tonight." She finished the last of her wine. "But I'd better get some rest so we can get to work tomorrow." She said goodnight and carried her glass to the kitchen.

I chose not to ask her what she meant by "get to work." After another hour or so, I finally climbed into bed. As Kit snuggled up under the covers next to me, I thought I'd never fall asleep with my mind humming from the events of the evening. Poor Martha.

◈⸻►►

A buzzing woke me. Hadn't I just fallen asleep? I squinted at the bedside clock, wondering why I'd set my alarm for so early. Oh, right. I was meeting Luke for a run. I threw on running clothes, changing my mind and my shirt three times, not that I wanted or needed to impress him. After settling on a Miles Davis tee, I pulled on a sweatshirt. I resisted the urge to put on mascara, though I did dab on a bit of strawberry lip gloss to protect my lips from chapping.

I tiptoed to Bobbie's room and pushed the door open. Kit slipped through and jumped on her bed, burrowing under the covers. Bobbie snorted and rolled over but didn't awaken.

After leaving Bobbie a note, I opened the front door, nearly turning back at the bleak sight of angry, gray skies. The winding road leading down the hill and into town disappeared into a misty cloud as I set off. I headed into the fog, a thin drizzle tickling my face.

When I arrived, I found Luke standing next to a huge chain-sawed carving of a bear next to the Grizzly Cafe. How could he look that good in baggy sweats?

"What, no dinosaur hat?" he teased.

"I had to turn it back in with the rest of the outfit." I feigned disappointment. "The Fossil Fest was quite an event. If this is what goes on in November, what does the town do for Halloween?"

"It's kind of low key, actually," he said. "The Fossil Fest is a scheme to get tourists to come up here during the slow season, so the businesses in town go all out."

"Whereas Halloween is a scheme for kids to get free candy?"

"Exactly." He gestured away from the main road. "There's a path that follows the river where I like to run.

Unless you had something else in mind." I gazed at the river trickling lazily downstream, gurgling like one of those meditation apps. All they did for me is make me want to pee.

"I don't recommend going that way." He pointed in the direction I'd been looking. "It used to be a great path, but now there's a rockslide blocking the way."

"Uh-huh." Everything seemed so temporary. One day you were on a path with everyone happily walking and running around you, and the next day you were buried under a pile of rocks.

"Something wrong?" Luke asked, concern in his voice.

"What?"

"You seem distracted."

I didn't want to talk about Martha's death, but in a town this small, he'd find out soon enough. "We found Martha last night in her basement. She's one of Bobbie's neighbors." I tried to think of the polite words to say, but instead I blurted out, "She was dead."

His mouth dropped open. "Dead? Martha Randall? How? Did she have a heart attack?"

"They're not sure exactly." I didn't want to be the source of any rumors, even though I was beginning to agree with Bobbie that what had happened to Martha wasn't an accident.

Luke sat down on a boulder. "I need a minute."

"Sure," I said. "You knew Martha?"

He wiped a tear away before he answered. "She was my music teacher at the academy. I took some private lessons from her, too. She was an awesome lady."

I nodded, even though I barely knew her. "She seemed nice." She didn't deserve to die.

He stared off into the trees, and I felt as if I were intruding on his memories. After a minute or so of silence aside from the sounds from the stream, the birds, and the rustling trees, he turned to me. "Are you still up for a run? We could make it another day."

"Lead the way. Unless you'd rather reschedule. I mean, I hardly knew her, but it sounds like you were close."

He didn't answer right away, as if not wanting to admit his feelings. "I don't know about you, but no matter what's going on in my life or in the world, a run always makes me feel better."

I followed him at a moderate pace along the single-lane blacktop road. Pine trees were ubiquitous at this altitude, and I heard a faint trickling sound from the river hidden behind thick foliage. In spring, after the snow melted, the river would be a rushing torrent surrounded by lush foliage, but I hoped to be back in L.A. by then if not sooner.

We'd been running about twenty minutes when barking sounded behind us. Luke stopped and turned back.

"Hey, little guy," he said, as Kit ran toward him, yapping her fool head off.

"Girl," I corrected. "Knock it off," I scolded as she danced around Luke.

"You know this dog?"

"Yeah," I admitted. "She lives with me and my grandma."

He laughed. "You make her sound like she's your roommate. What's her name?"

"Kit." I sighed. "She's never going to be able to keep up."

"She made it this far, so I wouldn't sell her short. Let's keep running and see how she does."

We headed along the river with Kit running alongside us, wagging her tail. We hadn't gone far when Luke slowed down. "I don't want to kill your dog. Maybe we should head back."

Kit stopped and sat with one paw raised, as if waiting to ask the teacher a question. Her tail swept back and forth on the ground, and I'm pretty sure she'd need a bath when we got home. I also knew I'd be the one stuck with the job. I scooped her up and tucked her under my arm.

"Do you mind if we walk back?" I asked. "I'm a little out of shape anyway. When you're on vacation, your whole routine goes out the window."

"Does that mean you won't be staying in town long?"

Did I hear disappointment in his voice? "I'll probably be stuck here until after New Year's." I realized how that must have sounded and tried to backtrack. "I mean, it's a great place to spend the holidays. I loved visiting here for Christmas when I was a kid, but I really want to get back to work."

The advantage of walking back was that we could talk, and we did our best to fill each other in on what we had been doing since we were kids. He'd studied hard and spent most of his free time writing and playing music and planned to build a recording studio as soon as he could raise enough funds.

I skimmed over my gymnastics career, figuring he knew the story already, and told him about parkour and how learning the skills required practically saved me.

"Parkour?" he asked.

"Mostly I do what's called free running, which evolved from parkour." He gave me a blank look, so I explained as succinctly as I could. "Parkour developed from military obstacle course training. The idea is to get from one point to another through all sorts of obstacles in the most efficient way possible."

"And what we're doing isn't free running?"

"Free running doesn't follow the easy path. You make your own path, jumping over whatever's in the way and throwing in flips and tricks. And, unlike gymnastics, there weren't any expectations. No one judged me the way they did when I trained for the Olympics, and most people thought it was pretty cool."

"It sounds cool," Luke said appreciatively. "Can you show me?"

I didn't like to show off, but I supposed I wanted to impress him. After scanning the territory, I put Kit down and took off on a run, jumping from boulder to boulder and doing a few flips along the way. The road ahead was carved into the cliff, and I ran up the wall of rock and flipped backwards, landing on my feet.

Luke laughed.

I put my hands on my hips. "What's so funny?"

Kit ran circles around me and jumped two feet off the ground.

"Do that flip thing again." He pulled his phone out of his pocket. "I'll take a video."

I must have been scowling because he added, "Please?"

Kit danced around me as I backed away. "If you trip me," I said to the dog, "you're getting the cheap kibble from now on."

I ran toward the rock wall with Kit alongside me and did another backflip.

"She did it again," he said. "You didn't tell me you had a stunt dog."

He showed me the video, and sure enough, that darned dog had done a backflip. It wasn't as impressive as mine, but not bad for a dog.

He quizzed me about Kit's background, which I knew next to nothing about.

I changed the subject. "I never knew there was such a thriving music scene up here. The Ukulele Ladies. The Tuba Boys."

"The Cougar Choir," he added.

"You're making that up."

"Nope, I wish. I have to run every time they head my way. Apparently, they like their men either young or rich. I may not have a lot of money..."

"But you're young. Good thing you're fast," I said, snickering.

"You have no idea."

We headed back toward town at a leisurely pace. "What's with this big competition?" I asked. "I know there's a cash prize, but from what my grandmother says, it sounds like they really take it seriously."

"That's an understatement. They'll do almost anything to win. Last year, someone put molasses in one of the Tuba Boys' instruments. It took a week to get it out, and from what I heard, on a warm day a little still oozes out of the valves."

"That sounds like a sticky situation."

He groaned.

We walked in silence while I decided if I should confide in him. As a local, he might have inside information, and I could use another opinion. "Bobbie thinks someone caused Rosa's accident just to hurt the Ukulele Ladies' chances."

"I've heard crazier ideas," he said. "Sounds like you don't agree."

"Old ladies fall sometimes. Heck, I tripped and fell down the stairs on set once, which was embarrassing." I'd done it more than once, but he didn't need to know that. "I laughed it off and told everyone I do all my own stunts. Rosa's lucky she didn't break a hip. Martha wasn't so lucky," I added without thinking.

He stopped. "What do you mean? I thought she had a heart attack."

"Maybe. But helped along by a dose of electricity." When his eyes widened, I explained how Bobbie and I had found her. "Seeing her lying on the basement floor was..." I nearly said "shocking," but realized that would be a poor choice of words. "It was disturbing, to say the least." I might never get the image of her damp, fuzzy slippers out of my mind.

Kit lagged behind, so I picked her up again. "Bobbie thinks someone engineered Martha's accident, but if so, they went to a lot of trouble."

"Your grandmother is something else."

"No kidding." Was I getting carried away by listening to Bobbie's theories? "She's always had a vivid imagination, and I think these online classes she's taking are giving her ideas."

"She's gone back to school?"

"Private investigator school." I waited for his reaction, and he didn't disappoint.

Luke began to laugh and kept laughing until he had me laughing too. After about a minute he composed himself, wiping a tear from his eye. "Your grandmother wants to be a PI? Like, open up an office and take on clients?"

"Can you imagine?" I shuddered, thinking about how my mother would take the news. We'd have to make sure she never found out.

He walked me back to the house. We stood by the door like we'd come home after a first date, both waiting to see if the other would make a move.

"Want to hang out on the patio?" I asked. "Bobbie makes a mean cup of coffee."

"I need a shower," Luke said.

"Oh, sure. Me too." It's not like I wanted him to kiss me when I was all sweaty, but I felt disappointed anyway. "I suppose I'll see you around." I turned to climb the porch stairs.

"I'm playing with some guys at Gypsy's Tavern on Wednesday," he said. "If you get a chance, stop by. Super low key."

I turned around, and seeing his grin, I could hardly say no. Not that I'd planned to.

"Sure. I'll see if I can make it."

"Great! The first set starts at nine, and maybe we can grab a drink after." He turned and jogged down the driveway, and I watched him run down the street until he was out of sight. I sighed and checked my chin for drool.

"As for you," I said, wagging a finger at Kit. "Don't you ever steal my thunder again." I opened the front door, and she rushed in and dashed from room to room searching for Bobbie, instead finding Mr. Whiskers and chasing him back under the sofa.

With that task accomplished, Kit planted her nose by the sliding glass door. I opened the door to the deck, and she scampered out.

"There you are, Kit," Bobbie said. "Where did you run off to, you little rascal?"

Chapter Eight

After a quick shower, I poured myself a cup of coffee and took it out to the deck. Bobbie, still in her robe and slippers with Kit fast asleep in her lap, held a pair of binoculars up to her face.

"Nice peepers," I said. "Were they a bonus when you signed up for the detective classes?"

She lowered the binoculars and narrowed her eyes. "I'm watching Martha's house. Getting a feel for the comings and goings so I can start narrowing down our list of suspects. How is Luke?"

"He's fine," I said, not wanting to go into detail. "But that dog is a showoff."

"Kit?"

Hearing her name, the dog lifted her head, looked around, and gave Bobbie's chin a quick lick before laying her head back down in exhaustion.

"Yes, Kit. She followed me. Do you know she can do a backflip?"

"That doesn't surprise me." She lifted the binoculars again, aiming them across the street. "Where did Angela say she got Kit again?"

"From a rescue organization," I said. "One that doesn't ask too many questions if you write them a big donation check."

"Is that true?" Bobbie asked.

"You know how she is. No problem too big that it can't be solved with money." No problem except me, her daughter. I preferred not to dwell on my relationship with my mother, mostly because it brought up painful emotions I did my best to keep buried.

"Maybe Kit was trained for one of those dog acts—like they have on TV talent shows," Bobbie suggested.

The same idea had occurred to me. "Then why did she end up at a rescue? Mom said they told her she's young —around two years old. Too young for retirement."

"Maybe she has a bad attitude and doesn't do what she's told," Bobbie said. "Sound like anyone you know?"

"I have no idea what you're talking about." Just because I wasn't Little Miss Sunshine didn't mean I had a bad attitude. I liked to think of myself as a pragmatist. "Why'd you never tell me you play the ukulele?"

She aimed the binoculars further up the road at a car headed our way. "I don't tell you everything." She tracked the car until it passed by.

Maybe I didn't want to know everything, but I didn't get why playing a wannabe guitar would be a secret. "How long have you been in the Ukulele Ladies? You have to be sixty-five to join, right?"

She set the binoculars next to her coffee cup. "I

applied the minute I was eligible, so it's been about five years."

I snickered. "Right. You can lie about your age to anyone else you want, but remember, I know how old you are."

"Fine. It was ten years ago," she admitted. "There were already five women in the group, and I made six. Alice passed away the following month, so we were back to being a quintet. We've been a quintet pretty much ever since."

"What about Ralph?"

"That's a funny story," she said. "Four or five years ago, his wife left him for some guy she dated in high school."

"That's not very funny."

She reached over and smacked me on the thigh. "The funny part is that Ralph took his wife's place in the group. He even fit into her shirt since she was quite buxom."

"Huh." Sometimes I didn't know what else to say.

"It's going to be different without Martha." She gazed into the forest and sighed.

"I'm sorry you lost your friend. I can only imagine how you must have felt seeing her like that."

She didn't answer right away. "If Rosa can't play with her injured wrist, we'll have to perform as a trio."

Obviously, she didn't want to talk about Martha now. Everyone grieved in their own way, and it might take weeks for Bobbie to process her feelings.

"It's really going to hurt our chances," she said. "Not that we were a favorite to win, but, as they say, hope springs eternal."

"Why is everyone so cutthroat about winning the competition? What's the big deal? Do they need the money that bad?"

"I don't think any of the musicians are desperate for their share of five thousand dollars—it would be less for each performer in the bigger groups. But Martha was really hoping we'd win. We don't—didn't—talk about money, but I could tell she was on a tight budget."

"Yeah, I got that feeling. That shag carpeting must be decades old."

She reached for her coffee and took a sip. "There's a lot of perks for the group that wins. You get to open for the headliner at the New Year's Eve show and hang out with them backstage. This year, it's Apollo and the Muses, so everyone is dying to get closer to them."

"I'm not sure that's the best choice of words," I said. When she gave me a puzzled look, I said, "Dying"?

"Oh, you know what I mean." She leaned forward in her chair and lowered her voice as if sharing a secret. "One of the Soul Sisters claimed she slept with Apollo."

"His name is really Apollo?"

She gave me a look as if she hadn't considered the question until now. "I suppose not, now that you mention it. Anyway, she's quite excited to see him again. And the Cougar Choir is a bunch of over-the-hill groupies. They'll sleep with anyone."

My grandmother had changed since my grandfather died, or maybe this was the real Bobbie coming out of her shell. "How many women are in the Cougar Choir? That is, if they are all women." If Ralph could be a Ukulele Lady, the possibilities were endless.

"I think they're down to just three or four members, and, yes, they are all women."

"Not much of a choir," I said.

"They started out with a dozen, but they don't always replace members when they leave. They allow membership at age fifty, so they have a lower mortality rate, but they require their members to be single or divorced, and they've lost a few who've gotten married."

"Can anyone form a group and join the competition?" I asked.

"It's open to any musical group with members from the community. Some of the groups have rules for their members, like we do, but all the performers have to live in Arrow Springs. One time, the Tuba Boys brought in a ringer with a fake I.D. Turned out he lived in Big Buck Springs."

"Yoo hoo," a voice called out from inside the house.

"Expecting someone?" I asked. "Or do neighbors just let themselves in whenever they feel like it?"

"It's Nancy. She has a key."

A woman in jeans and a zip-up sweatshirt stuck her head out of the patio door. Her thin, salt-and-pepper hair had been carefully styled into a limp bouffant. "Oh, there you are. I knocked, but no one answered the door, so I let myself in."

Bobbie waved the woman over. "This is Nancy. She helps me out with the housekeeping."

"Oh, you must be Whit. I've heard so much about you," Nancy said, and proceeded to inform me about everything she'd heard from my grandmother and others.

"I didn't live here when you were training for the Olympics. I'm so sorry about how that worked out."

"Thanks," I said, hoping she'd drop the subject. In L.A., people rarely asked about my ill-fated Olympic dreams, but during my brief stay with Bobbie, everyone I ran into wanted to rehash my painful past. I felt proud of how I'd come back from that low point in my life, but I still cringed when people brought it up.

"I can't believe what happened to Martha," Nancy said. "It was so sudden. Such a tragic accident."

"Yes, tragic," Bobbie said. She paused, glancing at me and back at Nancy as if deciding whether to confide her suspicions. "I don't think it was an accident."

Nancy sat on the edge of a chair and leaned forward eagerly. "What are you saying?"

"I'm saying she was murdered."

"She's saying she's going to let the police handle it," I said, hoping to keep the women from going rogue on me. "I'm sure they'll get to the bottom of it."

Bobbie gave me an annoyed glance and straightened in her chair, disturbing Kit, who had to rearrange herself to get comfortable. "I think it might be the same person who's responsible for Rosa's fall. Manny, Rosa's son, wants her out of the house badly, but I don't see any connection between him and Martha." She paused and I could see the wheels turning behind her steel-gray eyes.

Nancy's eyes widened. "You think Martha's death has something to do with Rosa's accident?"

Bobbie shrugged one shoulder and leaned back in her chair. "Maybe Martha knew something about Rosa's accident not really being an accident, and Rosa's son had to take her out."

I stood up, hoping to put a temporary halt to the wild speculation. "You've been watching reruns of America's Most Wanted again, haven't you?" I turned to Nancy. "Would you like some coffee?"

"Thanks, but I'd better get to work." Nancy turned back to Bobbie. "If you need someone to fill in until Rosa feels better, I've been practicing my ukulele. I've even watched videos online. I think I'm getting much better."

"That's lovely of you to offer, but I don't think we have time to break in a new member before the competition."

"Oh, of course," Nancy said, looking disappointed. "If you change your mind..."

I waited until Nancy had gone inside before speaking to my grandmother. "Why don't you let her play with you? I think she feels left out."

Bobbie gave me a willful look. "She's really terrible—can't keep time at all and messes everyone else up." Under my persistent glare, she softened. "Fine, I'll talk to the others. It's not just up to me, you know."

With Bobbie's strong personality, I had no doubt that the other Ukulele Ladies would go along with whatever she decided.

Chapter Nine

"What do you have planned for today?" I asked, thinking Bobbie might be planning to knit or bake to get her mind off Martha's death. I hoped for baking.

"I think I'll stop by John Chen's office. Want to come?"

"The real estate developer? Why? Are you thinking of selling your house?"

She scoffed. "You know he made an offer on Rosa's house. I think he wanted to buy Martha's house, too." She dropped Kit on my lap and went inside.

"Was it something I said?" I asked the dog, who tilted her head quizzically before curling up on my lap.

Twenty minutes later, Bobbie returned fully dressed in one of her flowy, hippy-dippy outfits and handed me a card.

"JRC Development LLC," I read aloud. "John Chen, President. Is this the card you got from Manny?"

"No, I found it at Martha's house. It's identical to the one Manny gave me."

"And you think he killed her to get her to sell? That makes no sense. Who knows how long it will take to settle the estate?"

"Maybe he didn't mean for her to die. Or maybe he's not in any hurry. Are you coming or not?"

I shook my head. "I'm going to follow up with the stunt coordinator. See if I can get some work."

"That's okay. It's not a long walk. Someone may drive by and take pity on an old lady."

When I got to be Bobbie's age, I planned to play the senior citizen card as much as I could. I tried to resist the guilt trip, but if something happened to her, not only would I feel horrible, but I wouldn't hear the end of it from my mother. As the black sheep of the family, I never thought I'd be the one keeping my grandmother out of trouble.

"Fine." I gave in. "I'll take you after I answer my emails. We can go somewhere for lunch afterwards."

When we were both safely buckled into the seats of my car, Bobbie announced she had a stop to make before we visited the real estate developer.

"Where to?" I asked, suspicious about why she hadn't mentioned it earlier.

"Arrow Investigations."

"Excuse me?"

"Ar-row In-vest-i-ga-tions," she repeated as if I were hard of hearing. "They're a private investigation firm."

"Yeah, I figured as much." I put the car in reverse and backed out of the driveway, heading in the direction she indicated. "Are you planning to hire them? The police are already looking into Martha's death. I don't know what you think a private detective will be able to find out that you haven't."

She gave me a smug smile. "I'm just doing a little reconnaissance."

"Oh, I see. You want to find out how a real-life PI operates? I'll tell you. Lots of boring computer work and following wayward spouses for hours hoping to catch them in an indiscretion. Doesn't sound like fun to me."

"I know all that. I'm not looking to be a PI for the glamour. Not that I'd mind a little excitement. Have you ever hung out with a bunch of old ladies? Most of them only want to talk about their aches and pains and their last doctor's visit. Or their next."

"You do know you're an old lady too, right?" I thought I might as well check.

"Of course, but I'm different. So are the rest of the Ukulele Ladies. That's why I'm discerning about who we let into the group. They say one bad apple doesn't spoil the whole bunch, but when you're around one complainer, it doesn't take long until everyone is moaning and groaning."

It seemed as if Bobbie had more excuses to keep people out of the group than she had reasons to let them join. I resolved to keep quiet on the subject.

We drove into town, passing by the community center, the general store, and all the touristy shops before veering off on a side road. I pulled into a strip mall parking lot where faded and peeling signs announced a liquor store, a pawn shop, and a sketchy-looking insurance agent among other fine establishments. If Arrow Springs had a bad side of town, I'd just found it.

I parked in front of a smoke shop specializing in vape products and CBD. Bobbie led me toward the stairs past a beauty salon where I could get a wash and cut for just fifteen bucks. I might have to come back when I had more time.

We climbed metal steps to the second floor where we emerged onto a dreary hallway. Stains covered the greenish-brown industrial carpet that led us to the doorway of Arrow Investigations. Bobbie knocked.

"Did you call and make an appointment?" I asked, confident I already knew the answer.

"Does this look like the office of an investigator who won't take walk-in business?"

"No, but he might be off playing golf or something."

"At the bar, more likely."

She tried the doorknob and pushed the door open. We stepped into a reception room about ten feet square where a secretary might have sat behind a desk to receive visitors. The desk was there, the sort a college student might squeeze into a dorm room. Stacks of paper covered most of the surface. If the PI did have a secretary, which I doubted, they had a lot of filing to catch up on.

"Look," I said, pointing to a door to the inner office. "Just like in the movies." The door had a frosted glass panel with stenciled-on letters: Bernard Fernsby, Private Investigator.

"Maybe he's in there and he's dead," Bobbie said as she moved closer to the door.

"That would be too much like the movies. Why don't you knock?"

Bobbie rapped gently on the wooden part of the door, and we were rewarded by the sound of a snort on the other side. Some rustling and grunting followed before the door opened.

A man stood in the doorway, thin strands of hair partially covering his nearly bald head. Untamed, shaggy eyebrows hovered above puffy eyes. Short and overweight by at least fifty pounds, he wore a rumpled shirt and gabardine pants. I recognized they'd once been good quality, but frayed cuffs told me they'd seen better days. Heck, he'd probably seen better days.

He cleared his throat. "Who are you?"

Not how I would have greeted a potential client, but I suspected we'd caught him off guard, possibly waking him up from a nap. The left side of his face had extra creases which matched his wrinkled shirt collar. His red nose made me wonder if he'd been drinking, and I reluctantly took a sniff of the air between us. I detected a slight scent of stale tobacco, but no bourbon or whiskey. Perhaps he was a vodka man. He seemed to have created a persona for himself, that of the grizzled PI, ready to take on the toughest cases.

Bobbie smiled, turning on the charm, a skill she'd mastered that I didn't share.

"Mr. Fernsby? My name is Roberta Leland. You may call me Bobbie." He gave her a blank look and stifled a yawn.

Bobbie forged on. "This is my granddaughter, Whitley. We'd like to discuss business with you if you're not too busy." She peered over his shoulder, and I followed her gaze into his office which held more stacks of paper.

"Bobbie Leland... are you by chance related to Phillip Leland of Leland Industries?"

She perked up at the mention of my father. "He's my son. My late husband started the business and Phillip took over upon his retirement."

Bernard's mood visibly brightened at this information. "Why don't I put on a pot of coffee, and we can talk while it's brewing. Come in." He stepped aside and motioned us to two chairs facing a battered wooden desk.

I took a seat, and while Bernard busied himself in the outer office, Bobbie gave the cluttered room a once-over, checking out the framed photos and an oak veneer bookcase. She pulled out a thick volume and blew a cloud of dust from the top before replacing it. When Bernard returned and took his place behind the desk, Bobbie took her seat next to me, her purse primly perched on her lap. After reaching into a drawer and retrieving a lined yellow pad, he addressed her. "Now, tell me about your situation."

"I am taking courses online through the Detective Training Institute of California and I need several thousand hours of experience to get my private investigator's license. I'd like to come work for you."

Chapter Ten

Bernard's face flushed and his mouth dropped open slightly. He cleared his throat again. "I'm not looking for a trainee. I can't even afford a secretary. You'd think spouses have quit cheating. Of course, the glory days were back in the sixties before they passed that blasted no-fault divorce law. Men would pay just about anything for pictures of their wives in compromising positions."

Bobbie shifted in her seat. "I think we're getting off the subject. I haven't yet mentioned that I would like to hire you to investigate a death. I'm quite sure it was murder, but I expect the police will rule it accidental."

"You don't know that," I said.

Bobbie ignored me. "Here's how I see it. I hire you to solve the case, and you hire me to assist you."

Bernard's eyes widened and he coughed. Then he wheezed and coughed some more.

"You really should consider quitting smoking," I said.

"Don't I know it." He stood up and asked us how we took our coffee before leaving the room. He returned with three mugs. Bobbie politely took a sip before placing it on a corner of the desk. I examined the muddy liquid and decided to pass.

They discussed the financial arrangements, which involved Bobbie being paid minimum wage while he would bill her double for her hours to cover overhead. It seemed a bit sketchy to me, but hopefully not illegal.

After finalizing those negotiations, Bernard took a big swig from his mug and smacked his lips with satisfaction. He picked up his pen, once again ready to take notes. "Start from the beginning."

Bobbie told him about the other women's accidents and then described in detail the scene we stumbled upon the night of Martha's death. "The police couldn't explain how the basement had flooded, nor how the wire came loose. I'm thinking someone flipped one of the breakers to lure her down there, knowing she'd be electrocuted the moment her feet touched the water."

He nodded. "Have you been able to get a copy of the police report?"

"They refuse to release it to me. According to Deputy Wallenthorp, it's an open investigation."

"I still have friends on the force," he said, making a note for himself on the yellow pad before mumbling, "At least I hope I do."

"When did you talk to the police?" I asked Bobbie.

"I called this morning while you were still asleep. What about the autopsy report?" Bobbie asked. "Can you find out the results?"

"That might take a few days. Have you been in touch with her family?"

Bobbie shook her head. "She has no family unless there are some distant grand-nieces or something. She didn't have any kids and she outlived the rest of her relatives, at least the ones I knew about."

"Do you have any evidence indicating foul play?" Bernard asked.

"No," Bobbie admitted. "That's why I'm here. I know in my bones it's murder." She paused to let that sink in. "I'd be interested in the results of a tox screen if they're doing one."

He nodded. "That's as good a place to start as any. I'll check in the morning."

"What do you want me to do?" Bobbie asked.

Without glancing up from his notes, he said, "You can begin with the filing."

Bobbie leaned forward in her chair as if wondering whether she'd heard him correctly. "Filing? You mean that mess in the front office?"

"Paperwork is very important in this business. Once you finish it, I'll find other tasks for you."

Bobbie didn't seem happy about the request, but she didn't argue as I might have done. "Fine." She stood and leaned over the desk to shake his hand. "Whit and I will start tomorrow."

I hoped I'd heard wrong. "Huh?" Part of the reason I'd become a stuntperson was to make sure I'd never have to do anything as tedious as office work.

Bobbie ignored me, arranging a time for us to return the following day.

I followed her out into the hallway. "I'm not filing."

"Then you can keep me company while I do the work. That's how it usually works, doesn't it?"

I had a feeling she'd snuck a dig in there, but I figured I'd wait for just the right time for my comeback. She wouldn't know what hit her.

We reviewed the plan to interrogate the real estate developer on the drive to his office. I hoped it would at least get us in the door.

I pulled the car into the parking lot next to a two-story angular building covered in redwood shingles. It didn't seem to know if it wanted to be modern or old-fashioned, and I said as much to my grandmother as we walked toward unit 121.

"Maybe it's like Donny and Marie," she said.

I stopped, wondering who and what she was talking about.

"You know. They're a little bit country and a little bit rock and roll."

Sometimes, it's better not to ask, so I headed toward the big sign that read JRC Developers LLC.

I held the door open for Bobbie and followed her into a small reception area where a woman sat behind a desk talking on the phone. She appeared to be around my age, with a no-nonsense approach to fashion, right down to her ponytail and rosy cheeks. She didn't fool me. It took work to look like you woke up like that.

She hung up and eyed us curiously. "May I help you?"

"I hope so. I'm Bobbie Leland, and this is my grand-daughter, Whitley."

"Whitley?" she repeated tentatively. "You used to go to gymnastics camp every summer, didn't you?"

I nodded and prepared myself for the inevitable questions.

Instead, she squealed and ran around the desk, grabbing me in a hug. "It's me, Jenna! I used to follow you around all the time."

"Oh, sure." I plastered on a smile even though I had no idea who she was. I figured it would save time if I played along.

"I'm not surprised you don't remember me. I was three years younger than you back then. Still am, come to think of it." She guffawed at her own joke.

I took a closer look as she eyed me reverently. Sandy brown hair, freckles, little button nose. "Did you ask me for my autograph once?"

"I still have it." She grinned. "Have you moved here? Maybe we can go out for drinks sometime."

"Sure," I said, hoping she wouldn't follow through. I had enough friends, which is to say none. I liked it that way. I had coworkers and acquaintances, which worked out fine for me. Friends always wanted to borrow things, like your favorite jacket or your boyfriend, and sooner or later they wanted to bore you with all their personal problems.

"Jenna." Bobbie interrupted our little one-way love fest. "We're here to see Mr. Chen. Is he in?"

"Yes. Let me tell him you'd like to see him." She slipped into one of the offices toward the back of the space and returned moments later. "You can go in now."

An enormous oak desk filled the small room, dwarfing

the man seated behind it. His eyes were magnified behind wire-rimmed glasses.

He motioned for us to sit across from him. "How may I help you lovely ladies today?"

Bobbie gave me a smirk before explaining she wanted to sell her house. "I understand you're interested in buying houses in town."

"Just one," he said. "My mother is getting older, and I'd like to have her close by. I showed her pictures of homes on the market, but none of them appealed to her, so I made inquiries with a few residents. She's rather old fashioned and doesn't care for the mountain cabin style that's so prevalent in our town."

Bobbie nodded. "Well, that explains why you've never expressed interest in my house."

"And which house is that?"

"I'm across the street from Martha Randall. I understand you made her an offer."

"An inquiry," he corrected. "She mentioned it to you?"

"Oh, yes. She seemed quite interested at the time."

His face fell. "Is she no longer interested?"

"You could say that." Bobbie scooted forward in her seat. "You see, she's dead. I thought you might know something about her accident."

He pulled back as if he'd been accused of something, which wasn't far from the truth. "How would I possibly know?"

I decided it was time to jump in. "My grandmother was good friends with Martha, so naturally she's very upset."

He scowled at me before turning to Bobbie. "Are you

really in the market to sell your house? Or have you come here to waste my time?"

I spoke before Bobbie could say something we'd both regret. "You're obviously not interested in buying Bobbie's house, so we'll get out of your hair." I pushed my chair back and stood, adding, "Sorry to have bothered you."

Motioning to Bobbie that we were leaving, I headed for the door, hoping she was right behind me.

As we passed by Jenna's desk, she waved me over. In not much more than a whisper, she said, "Mr. Chen couldn't possibly have been involved with Martha's death." When I raised my eyebrows, she added, "I overheard you talking."

Bobbie came closer and in a soft voice, asked, "How do you know this?"

"That day, when Martha died, we were both here all day until six o'clock. He didn't even go out for lunch." She paused and added in a louder voice, "Don't forget about those drinks. First round is on me."

"Oh, sure," I said, noncommittally.

As soon as we were outside, Bobbie said, "That was a waste of time."

"Not really," I said. "At least now you know he's not involved. We can start focusing on other suspects."

"We?" She stopped walking and gave me a hopeful look.

I stopped too. I hardly knew Martha, but I did know she was a nice lady who didn't deserve to die. It didn't seem right that someone should get away with murder just because she didn't have relatives to make a big stink and badger the police to find the truth. And on top of it, until we knew who killed Martha and why, I wasn't sure Bobbie was safe, not to mention the rest of the women in town.

"Come on," I said, motioning her to pick up her pace. "We've got a murder to solve. But first, let's get lunch."

Chapter Eleven

Wen Bobbie told me where we were having lunch, I had high hopes, thinking she'd said "Gastronome," which means fancy, expensive food, or something like that. When I pulled into the parking lot, I stared at the sign incredulously. Gastro Gnome. A gnome-themed restaurant?

Ceramic bearded men and buxom women with tall red hats surrounded the building. I knew they were going to invade my dreams tonight, and the thought gave me a little shiver.

Once inside, the little statues were everywhere. I had just resolved to avoid eye contact with any mythical creatures when I spotted the greeter coming our way. He wore authentic peasant wear and a big pointy red hat.

Thankfully, the menu, while full of gnome puns like "Gnome-gnomes" for appetizers, offered typical coffee shop food.

After we ordered sandwiches and iced tea, I asked

about Martha's lack of relatives. "She must have a will. Who did she leave her house to?"

"Good question. I'll ask Bernard to look into it."

"Speaking of relatives," I began. I'd been wanting to ask her about Julia, my birth mother, ever since I saw the picture on her mantel.

"Yes?" She smiled, but I sensed tension as if she knew what I wanted to ask.

"Has my mother been in touch? I mean Julia, not Angela," I clarified.

"Why do you ask?"

"I saw the picture on the mantel. It looks recent."

She reached out for my hand, but I pulled it back and put it in my lap.

I pressed my fingernails into my palms as my anger rose. "Tell me."

She sucked in a deep breath, then closed her eyes as she slowly released the air from her lungs. "Your mother—that is, Angela—doesn't want me talking to you about her." Her eyes tightened, reminding me that I wasn't the only one affected by Julia's actions. When my birth mother gave me up and returned to South America, not only had I lost a mother, but Bobbie had lost a daughter.

Now I reached across the table and took her hand, which felt fragile in mine. Bobbie was my rock, but maybe she wasn't as strong as I thought she was.

I leaned forward and quietly said, "I won't tell Angela. You know I won't."

Bobbie looked down at her hand and said one word. "Ow."

Letting go of her hand, I laughed. "I guess I don't

know my own strength." How could I make her tell me what I wanted to know? "I can take the truth, no matter what it is."

She nodded, staring at her plate and the half-eaten sandwich. "She sent me a letter a few months ago along with the picture. In some ways, she hasn't changed a bit. Older, of course, but still a beautiful girl."

"A beautiful woman," I corrected. "Is she still in South America?"

"Yes. She looks happy, doesn't she?"

Her words stabbed me through the heart, and I swallowed hard. "She does. Is she ever coming back?"

Bobbie pushed her plate off to the side. "Maybe. Someday. When it's safe."

"Why wouldn't it be safe for her to come home?"

"Not for her," she said, pausing and looking me straight in the eye. "For you."

"What does that mean?" I was going to get the truth from her that I'd waited for so long. The real reason she gave me up and left the country.

Bobbie shook her head slowly. "She never told me."

I didn't believe that for a moment, but before I could press her, we were interrupted.

"Well, hello ladies." Ralph stood next to the table, holding a ball cap in his hands. "Do you mind if I join you?"

"We're about to leave," I said, annoyed by his timing.

"Whit!" Bobbie scolded. She turned back to Ralph. "Of course, you can join us. Have a seat."

"No, if you're done eating... Another time. It's just so sad about Martha. I wanted to see how you're taking it."

Now I felt like a heel. I stood up and gestured to my seat. "Have a seat. I'm sure you and Bobbie have a lot to talk about. I'll check my email and be back shortly." When I'd had time to digest the bombshell about my birth mother, I'd bring it up again, but for now I felt emotionally wrung out.

Once outside, I checked my phone. I found a second email from the stunt coordinator who said shooting on the new project wouldn't start until after the first of the year. "I'll let you know," she wrote.

I paced in the parking lot, not wanting to intrude on Bobbie and Ralph's conversation. Bobbie acted tough, but I knew she had a gooey center, like chocolate lava cake. It was one of the things I appreciated most about her.

When I returned to our table, Ralph had left. "What are our plans for the rest of the day?"

"Didn't I tell you?" she asked innocently. "There's a meeting this afternoon at the community center for all the competition entrants. I thought it would be a good chance to investigate the other musicians and see if we can flush out some more suspects."

"What time is the meeting?" I glanced at the wall where the clock gnome was pointing at the one and the six.

"It starts at two o'clock," Bobbie said. "We'll be right on time if we don't dawdle."

"Got it," I said. "Ix-nay on the awdle-day."

"You still speak in pig Latin." Bobbie beamed as if I'd shown fluency in actual Latin.

"Being around you makes me revert to being a child. Especially when you say things like 'don't dawdle.'"

"Finish your vegetables and let's get going."

I looked at what was left of my BLT and the mound of coleslaw on the plate. Popping the last piece of bacon in my mouth, I asked, "What about dessert?"

"Some gnome-made cookies, perhaps?" Bobbie suggested with a smirk.

I responded with a groan.

She called the server over and asked for the check and two brownies to go. As soon as he brought our sweets, Bobbie put a twenty and a ten on the table, and I marveled that there were people who still used cash.

I grabbed the bag from Bobbie as we headed for the door, taking a big bite of chocolatey goodness. With one last look around, I vowed never to step foot inside the Gastro Gnome restaurant again if I could help it.

The last time I'd visited Arrow Springs, the new community center was all everyone talked about. It had taken years for the white block building to get approved and built, and now it was the pride of the town. It was sleek and modern without the slightest hint of personality.

In the cavernous lobby, a middle-aged woman behind a faux-marble information counter smiled expectantly. I took a step in her direction, but Bobbie grabbed my elbow and pulled me down a wide hallway.

"We're meeting in room twelve," she said.

We stepped inside the room which held about a hundred folding chairs lined up in neat rows. Along the back, a table had been set up with a coffee urn and other drinks. I grabbed a bottle of water and Bobbie filled a Styrofoam cup with coffee and powdered creamer.

As she stirred her coffee with a plastic stick, she

surveyed the room, no doubt looking for her next interrogation subject. Spotting her target, she bustled toward a group of three women near the front of the room who appeared a decade or two younger than her.

Bobbie greeted them with air kisses and introduced me to the Soul Sisters. Felicia and Vanessa were retired professional backup singers who'd worked at Motown in the late sixties and seventies before moving to Los Angeles and focusing on session work.

"Session work was steadier during the eighties and nineties, and you didn't have to travel," Felicia explained. "That's a big plus when you're raising a family. Then the work gradually dried up. No matter how good you sing, it's hard to compete with younger singers."

"Ain't that the truth," Vanessa said.

"For a while, we had a lounge act. We got a gig at the Peak Experience one summer, and we fell in love with the place. I divorced long ago, so when Vanessa's husband passed away, we moved up here, joined the church choir, and that's where we met Deb."

The blonde gave me a little wave. "That's me."

Vanessa gently touched Bobbie's arm. "I'm so sorry about Martha. What a sweet lady."

The other two women joined in with their condolences while I stood by awkwardly.

"How is Rosa?" Felicia asked.

"She's home from the hospital," Bobbie said. "I don't know how soon she'll be able to play her ukulele. She injured her wrist."

There was a lot of tsk-tsk-ing, and one "poor thing."

"It's almost like the Ukulele Ladies are cursed," Deb said.

Vanessa gasped. "Don't say that. Not out loud. Remember the snake I found in my bathtub? Maybe the entire competition is cursed."

Bobbie lowered her voice. "I don't think what's been happening is because of any curse. And I don't think they were accidents either."

Before the others could ask Bobbie what she meant, a voice came over the P.A. system, announcing the start of the meeting.

"We'd better find a seat," I told Bobbie. The first few rows had filled up since we'd arrived. We passed by a trio of mature women wearing tight-fitting animal print dresses and leggings with high heels.

I nudged Bobbie. "Is that the Cougar Choir?"

"Not hard to pick out, are they?" She led me to where Gypsy had saved us spots.

"I hear you've been doing some bartending," Gypsy said. "I'm going to need some help over the holidays if you're still in town. Come on down to the Tavern one evening, and we'll talk."

"Sounds great." I could use a few extra bucks.

"And you missed rehearsal this morning," Gypsy said to Bobbie. "Will you be there tomorrow? My house, nine a.m."

Bobbie's lips pressed together in a slight grimace. "Sorry, I have some important business to attend to."

A man sitting in the row in front of us turned around and shushed us. A tiny woman stood behind the podium, attempting to get the room's attention. She wore a pastel pantsuit that hung loosely on her petite frame, and her silver hair stuck to her head in tiny curls.

"That's Alice," Bobbie whispered. "She's the mayor's secretary."

Alice craned her neck to reach the microphone and went over the rules for the contest, which consisted of a dress code that encouraged family-friendly costumes. The Cougar Choir didn't appear to take the announcement well, and I scanned the room to see the others' reactions. I became so interested in people watching, I forgot to listen to the speaker.

"What?" Bobbie cried out as she jumped to her feet.

"What?" I wondered what I'd missed.

"I said," Alice repeated, "Each group will consist of four to ten performers."

"Since when?" Bobbie demanded, then turned to me. "That's it," she said, loud enough for the whole room to hear. "Someone is trying to sabotage us!"

The noise level in the room rose as murmurs turned into shouting. Poor Alice tried to restore order as she called out over the P.A. "Quiet, everyone. Quiet."

Observing the attendees, I noticed a few surprised faces while others angrily argued with anyone nearby. A group of six men a few rows ahead of us wearing jackets embroidered with "Phil R. Monics" found the incident amusing. They ranged from middle-aged on up, with one man who must have been in his nineties.

The disturbance showed no sign of resolving itself, and I didn't want to spend my entire day at the community center, so I stood, put two fingers in my mouth, and whistled. That startled everyone, and they stopped talking long enough for me to call out, "Alice has something to say. Bobbie will be available after the meeting to take your questions." I sat down so Alice could continue.

"Thank you, dear," Bobbie said.

Alice continued with the rules and moved on to the rehearsal schedule, which brought on more disorder, since many attendees weren't happy with their allotted time slots.

"I heard one of the Cougar Choir is sleeping with the mayor," one woman called out from the back of the room.

"I'd like to know which one," another voice countered.

I looked over at the Cougars, who wore smug smiles, not exactly the picture of innocence.

Bobbie leaned closer and said, "We don't have to stay. I think I've heard enough."

"But I told everyone you'd take questions later."

She stood and put a hand on one hip. "You can stay if you like, but I'm going."

⁂

We got back to the house in time for me to practice my mixology skills before dinner. Bobbie made a great test subject for my recipes, as long as I didn't mind her oddball comments.

I mixed up a couple of classic old fashioneds, garnished with lemon peel. I handed one to Bobbie, and she took a tentative sip.

"Is this a Manhattan?" she asked.

"Old Fashioned. We're out of vermouth. This uses Angostura bitters and muddled sugar." If coaxed I could go into a treatise about the history and traditions behind both drinks, but I decided to wait for a more appreciative audience. "Do you like it?"

"I think I do." She took another sip. "Yes, I definitely do."

My phone vibrated and the screen showed way too many unread emails. Hopefully, none of them were urgent.

While I sipped my drink, I deleted email after email before coming to one from a colleague named Madison. I'd shown her the ropes on one of her first gigs a few years earlier. Her email said a stunt coordinator I knew only by reputation needed someone for a short-term job and asked if I might be interested.

I emailed her back to let her know I was interested, trying not to sound desperate, which isn't easy when you are, in fact, desperate.

Another email from an actor I'd worked with on my last set caught my attention. She was looking for a room-mate and heard I might be looking for a place.

I'm enjoying my break in the mountains, I typed, leaving out the part about the break not being voluntary, *but I can't wait to get back to L.A.*

"Must be good news," Bobbie said.

I looked up, guessing she'd caught me smiling. "Potentially. I have a good feeling about it."

The phone rang—an L.A. number I didn't recognize.

"Hey, Whitley, it's Madison. I figured I'd go old school and give you a call."

"Hey, Madison." I hoped she called about the job, but

I figured I'd let her bring it up. Better not to seem too eager.

"I was kinda surprised to hear you're still in the biz. Haven't heard your name mentioned since Legends of the Defenders got cancelled. Must be a drag to have to look for work after being on a series for five years."

"Yeah, but we knew it was coming." I'd spent months getting myself out of a funk after losing that job, and I wasn't about to get depressed about it all over again. "I figured I'd take some time off."

There was a moment of silence, and I looked at the phone screen to make sure we hadn't been disconnected. Phone service could be sketchy in the mountains.

"I heard there was an incident on set," she said. "With the director."

"Oh that." I tried to sound nonchalant. "All the women in Hollywood should thank me for putting him in his place."

"Unfortunately, men still run the studios, pretty much."

I didn't like the direction this conversation was going, and my kind and gentle facade was beginning to wear thin. "Was there a reason you called besides explaining the patriarchy to me?"

She laughed softly, but I couldn't tell if she was laughing with me or at me.

"One of the doubles got pregnant, and they're going to need someone to take her place at least until after she has the baby. And who knows? She might not come back. She's around your size, so I thought of you. Are you free for lunch on Thursday?"

"Sure, no problem." I didn't need to tell her I was two or three hours away from L.A.

"You know, your social media is a wasteland. You might get more work if you posted. People forget about you quickly in this biz."

Being on a long-running series was great, but it meant I'd gotten out of the habit of networking. Getting work depended on connections, and mine had dried up.

We set up a time and place to meet and I hung up the phone. I took a quick look at a couple of my social media accounts. Madison was right. I hadn't posted in months. Well, that was easy to fix. Maybe I could get Luke to take some shots for me. In the meantime, I posted the video of Kit doing her back flip.

There was one person I had to contact, and I couldn't put it off any longer. I'd ignored the texts from Kyle, my ex-boyfriend, asking me when I was going to get the rest of my stuff out of his apartment.

Kyle had thrown me out on the street after our last fight. Not literally on the street, of course, since I managed to talk my mother into letting me stay at the beach house, but it still hurt. I sent him a message letting him know I could stop by Thursday for my things. He immediately texted back, asking if he could take me out for a drink. He said he was hoping we could talk.

My stomach did a little flip-flop. I wondered what he wanted to talk about. Did he miss me? Was he having second thoughts? I told my overactive imagination to knock it off. It was probably just something mundane like how much I still owed on the water bill or something like that. But that's not the sort of thing you discuss over drinks. Or was it?

Bobbie turned on the television. "What should we watch?"

I was too excited to sit around watching Murder She Wrote reruns, which was Bobbie's favorite. "I think I'll swing by Gypsy's Tavern. Might as well talk to Gypsy about doing some bartending while I'm there. I doubt I'll get back to my real job until after New Year's. Things really slow down this time of year."

"Good. Idle hands are the devil's workshop," Bobbie said.

"The Bible recommends tending bar?"

"That quote actually originates from Chaucer, not the Bible."

"Okay, then. See you later." Now I had another useless piece of trivia taking up valuable space in my brain. But she did have a point. It would be good to have something else to do besides sitting on the deck all afternoon followed by an evening of TV. I might as well make a few bucks until I got my career back on track.

After stuffing my phone and keys into my pockets, I opened the front door. "Did you know it was raining?"

"Is it?" Bobbie called back from her warm, comfortable spot. "Well, a little water never hurt anyone."

I closed the door and plopped on the sofa next to her. "Maybe. But why take the chance? I can go to Gypsy's another night."

Chapter Twelve

When I awoke the next morning, I heard ukulele music coming from Bobbie's bedroom. It didn't sound half bad. I tapped on her door and let her know I was headed to the gym.

The Arrow Springs Fitness Club didn't boast a lot of amenities, but it had a passable weight room, which I often had to myself as I did that morning. I went through my regular workout and in the middle of my last set of pullups, Jenna walked in. I held back a groan, nodding in response to her cheerful greeting.

Watching her from the corner of my eye, I expected to see her pick up some ten-pound dumbbells and do a few curls, but she'd obviously been shown the ropes. I watched her bench press what looked like around eighty pounds. Not as much as I could lift, but not bad for an amateur.

If I stuck around, she might want to chat, so I skipped the rest of my workout. I headed for the shower, relieved when Jenna didn't follow me to the locker room.

I'd just finished dressing when Jenna appeared around the corner, startling me.

"Hi." She didn't wait for a response. "Great workout. Want to meet again on Friday?"

I fought the urge to roll my eyes. "Actually, I prefer to work out alone. It's easier to concentrate that way."

"Oh, sure," she said, her smile fading. "Me too. I just thought if you needed someone to spot you... I guess I'll see you around."

"See you." I grabbed my bag and left.

When I got home, I found Bobbie dressed and ready to go. We arrived at Bernard Fernsby's office promptly at ten a.m. with coffee and donuts. Coffee was Bobbie's idea, and the donuts were mine. I polished off a Boston cream on the way.

We entered the front office without knocking, and I regarded the piles of papers on the desk with dread. They seemed to have grown overnight. Bobbie knocked on Bernard's door, and as she delivered coffee and donuts to him, I took a seat behind the desk and spun around in the chair a few times. When I got bored with that, I leafed through a stack of file folders mindlessly until I recognized a name on one.

A few photocopies clipped into the left side of the file showed the aftereffects of a fire. I paged through the notes on the right. Providential Mutual Insurance had hired Bernard to investigate the fire at Gypsy's Tavern. The fire investigator ruled the incident arson due to traces of an accelerant, and the insurance company didn't want to pay if Gypsy had engineered the fire.

Based on lack of evidence or motive, Bernard had

concluded that Gypsy wasn't responsible, and the case was closed. He never did find out who was responsible, but then, that's not what they'd hired him to do.

Maybe Bobbie had been right all along, and Rosa's fall wasn't an accident, either. But were these events connected to Martha's death?

Bobbie emerged from Bernard's office with a paper for me to sign. "It's a nondisclosure agreement, in case you come across any confidential information while you're watching me work."

"I already have." I showed her the file on the investigation of Gypsy's fire.

She leafed through the pages. "Arson." She gave me an "I told you so" look.

"I know. I guess there's more to these accidents than we'd... um, I'd thought. What I'm wondering is whether the same person engineered Martha's so-called accident. Maybe she wasn't supposed to die."

She raised one eyebrow. "Sure seemed to me like they wanted her dead."

I glanced at the form she handed me and scribbled my signature. Bobbie found some folders and began going through the stacks of papers, while I read an old, battered copy of Forensics magazine.

"Are you really going to read while I work?" Bobbie asked.

"This might come in handy someday. It's by some pollen expert. Did you know you can sometimes tell where a crime happened based on pollen and spores that get transported along with the body?"

"Fascinating. If you're going to sit there and read, why

don't you take a look at some of these papers? I'm separating them into piles of invoices, contracts, notes, and reports." She handed me a two-hole punch and instructed me on its usage.

"I know how to punch holes." I picked up a glamour photo of a middle-aged blonde. "Where does this go?"

She took the picture from me. "Why does Mr. Fernsby have a picture of Sheila? It must be at least ten years old." She flipped it over and read aloud, "Sheila M. Brockerson, 2010." She stared at it for at least a minute, then placed it back on the table.

"Sheila?" I asked. "Is that the non-friend of yours who left town?"

"It is. I'll have to ask Mr. Fernsby about her."

Bobbie spent the rest of the morning filing while I stacked papers, reading the ones that seemed interesting. Most didn't. She made surprisingly quick work of the job and had the desk cleared off by lunchtime.

"I'll go wake up Bernard," she said. "Why don't you make a pot of coffee?"

Bobbie knocked on his door, then entered the inner office while I threw some coffee grounds into a filter and started the machine brewing. The two of them emerged shortly, and Bernard stared at the desk as if he couldn't believe his eyes.

"Everything is filed?"

"It is," Bobbie assured him.

"I watched her do it," I said, just in case he thought she'd thrown everything in the trash. "I even helped." The look Bobbie gave me prompted me to add, "A little."

"I'll get us some lunch," Bobbie said, "and we can talk about my first assignment. Solving Martha's murder."

Bernard winced, but quickly recovered. "The Mexican joint downstairs has surprisingly good food. I'll take two crispy chicken tacos with a side of guacamole." He reached for his wallet, but Bobbie waved him off.

She handed me two twenties. "I'll take the same."

Before I could object to being the delivery girl, Bobbie and Bernard went into his office and closed the door.

The taco joint, a hole in the wall with a few tables and chairs, seemed promising based on the long line, not to mention the delicious aroma. When I finally reached the front of the line, the woman at the counter greeted me in Spanish. One of these days, I'd have to learn to say more than "No hablo español." I gave her the order, including extra guacamole for me, and took a seat to wait.

Several minutes later, she called my number, and I collected the food and carried it upstairs. We set up around Bernard's desk and I handed Bobbie her tacos.

"Thank you, dear." She used a napkin as a placemat on the edge of the desk, laying her tacos out neatly. "Do you remember I told you that Sheila left town?"

"Um, sure." I couldn't be expected to remember everything she told me, could I?

"Just last week, one of the members of the Cougar Choir hired Mr. Fernsby to track her down."

My brain cells started working. "But didn't you say she'd gone to visit her daughter?"

"That's what I'd been told. According to Mr. Fernsby, Sheila sent out a text to all her contacts saying she didn't know how long she'd be gone. The other Cougar Choir members thought it was odd, but they couldn't get the police to investigate it. So, one of them finally gave up and hired Mr. Fernsby."

I turned to Bernard. "Do you think there's anything to it?"

"He took the case," Bobbie said before Bernard could answer.

"That doesn't necessarily mean anything," I said. "Why would he turn down a job if someone wants to hire him?" Maybe he wanted something else to do besides napping all day. "No offense," I said to Bernard.

"None taken," he said. "I've just started looking into it, and your grandmother has agreed to assist me on the case."

"Oh, she has, has she?" I pulled Bobbie aside. "I thought we were looking into Martha's death. Don't you want to find out who killed her?"

Bobbie's eyes widened. "You think I don't?"

"I think you've got this fantasy in your head about being a private investigator and chasing bad guys around or something."

"What's wrong with that?" she asked.

I stared at her for several seconds. "I thought you cared, but this is all just a game to you." Before she could respond, I shoved the door open, stomped out, and headed for the car.

I drove out of the parking lot, my heart beating hard in my chest. My trigger temper often got me in trouble, but I felt justified this time. As my feeling of superiority began to wear off, I wished life came with a rerun button. Had I really told Bobbie she didn't care?

As I contemplated how to get my mind off Bobbie and

our squabble, I decided working on my flips and tricks would help me get my focus back.

I found the number for the Universal Gymnastics Center where I'd trained as a kid. When the woman who answered heard my name, she said she'd be delighted for me to stop by and use the facilities.

I parked in the nearly empty parking lot and sat in my car, reconsidering. I hadn't been inside the building since I got kicked off the Olympic team. "Oh, grow up," I told myself. The moment I stepped through the doors and into the once-familiar space, I felt my stomach tighten. I hesitated in the silent room until I breathed in the smell of sweaty feet, chalk dust, and rubber mats. It felt like home.

Carol emerged from her office, introducing herself as the center's current owner. "Before I let you get to it, have you ever considered teaching or coaching? I could really use someone like you for the summer. Plenty of parents would love to have their kids train with an Olympic level athlete."

"I'm just here for the holidays," I said. "I'm a stunt-woman now."

"Yes, I heard. Still, you never know what life has in store for you, do you?" She let me know she'd be in her office if I needed her.

Working at a gymnastics center wouldn't be terrible, but I wanted my life back. If I couldn't be a stuntwoman, what was I? Just a has-been gymnast who almost made it. Few people other than those in the gymnastics world like Carol remembered my name. At the studios, I was among the best, just beginning to make a name for myself. I wasn't about to give up on my goals.

Once I'd taken off my shoes and walked on the cushioned floors, I felt like a kid again. I hopped up on the balance beam, walking back and forth to get my bearings. It seemed smaller somehow. Once I felt comfortable, I did a handstand and a few cartwheels. I'd have to get more practice in before doing handsprings or leaps.

Next, I chalked my hands and hit the uneven bars. It had always been my favorite event, and the one I scored highest on. It was the closest thing to flying I'd found. Soaring through the air, my mind focused on nothing else until I nailed my landing.

Two hours later, I checked my phone and saw a text from Bobbie asking me to pick her up. I smiled, hoping that meant she wasn't too mad at me. On the way out, I stopped by Carol's office to thank her.

"Come back anytime," she said. "And don't forget my offer."

As I drove to Bernard's office, I considered apologizing for my outburst, not sure if I wanted to. Bobbie waited for me by the parking lot. She got in the car, and didn't mention me storming out, so I figured I wouldn't either. Instead, I told her about Carol's suggestion. "Can you imagine me with a bunch of kids?"

I glanced over in time to see a goofy smile on her face, which she quickly hid. "No, not at all."

When we got home, Bobbie made a vegan chickpea stew. She served it in bowls over rice, and I had to admit it wasn't half bad. I even had seconds.

"I'm going to Gypsy's later to see Luke's band," I said as I helped clean up. "And maybe talk to Gypsy about bartending. Wanna come?"

She shook her head. "Have fun. I'm planning to go to bed soon so I can get up early and start working on Martha's case."

I took another shower, tried to do something with my hair, and said goodnight to Bobbie. Just before nine p.m., I walked into Gypsy's Tavern. Booths lined the right wall, and a long oak bar took up most of the left side. The place smelled like old grease and stale beer, just the way it did when I was a kid.

As a kid, when I stayed with my grandparents for the summer, they brought me here often, and we always sat at the last booth. I would order a burger and grape soda and pretend not to notice while the adults got drunk on margaritas. Bobbie and Gramps never made me feel like the kid they dragged along because they were too cheap to hire a babysitter.

At the back of the room, a small makeshift stage was set up, and a saxophone leaned against a stand—most likely Luke's.

There was someone sitting in my booth. I knew it didn't belong to me, but I still felt annoyed. The woman's back faced me, but I recognized the perky ponytail. Jenna. I considered leaving before anyone noticed me, but first, I quickly scanned the room. Luke stood at the bar. In that moment of indecision, he saw me.

His huge grin gave me a warm feeling down to my knees. "Hey, Whit," he said casually. "You made it."

"Hey, Luke."

Jenna's head whipped around, and instead of the welcoming smile I expected, I saw something predatory in her eyes. She popped out of her booth and ran over to Luke's side.

"Here, let me help you with those," she said, and took one of the draft beers the bartender had just poured. She stood close enough to Luke that their arms touched. "Hi, Whitley," she said, with a smug smile.

What was going on? Was Luke dating Jenna?

"Do you want to sit with us?" Luke asked. "I've got another ten minutes until the next set."

Before I could answer, Jenna said, "Oh, I'm sure she doesn't want to sit with us, Luke. No one likes to be a third wheel."

He gave her a confused look, so I decided to give her a chance for her to pull her claws in. I didn't want to have to make small talk with a woman who wanted to either stalk me or stake me.

"Thanks, I'm good." I reached for a barstool before Luke could object.

I slid onto the stool and observed the bartender washing glasses with his back to me. Medium height, strong shoulders, dark skin—Gypsy's son, Elijah, the hot guy I'd last seen wearing a dashiki.

"What can I get you?" he asked, startling me.

"You have eyes in the back of your head?"

He turned around. "Either that, or I can look in the mirror with the two on the front of my head." He motioned to the mirror on the back wall.

"Oh, right." *Smarty pants.* It sounded just as juvenile in my mind as it would have out loud. "I'll have an old fashioned, if you don't mind."

"I don't mind." He plopped a sugar cube into a glass and added bitters and a little water, which he muddled, just the way I would have done.

He put the drink down in front of me and waited for me to take the first sip.

"Wow, that's good," I said. "That's not well bourbon. What's that going to set me back?" I hoped I delivered the line with a playful tone, so he didn't think I was a cheapskate. I wasn't sure why I cared what he thought.

"On the house." He smiled, and it seemed flirtatious, but that might have just been my imagination. Or maybe, that was his way of getting better tips. I'd heard it could work.

"What brings you to this dive?" He leaned against the counter behind him, looking as relaxed as a tomcat who'd been fed for the day.

"I came by to see Luke play. I've known him since I was a kid." I stopped myself before over-explaining and telling him we were just friends.

He nodded and watched me take another sip of my drink. "How'd Bobbie ever talk you into leaving sunshine and ocean waves to come to Arrow Springs just when we're about to get below freezing weather? I've never known anyone to complain about spending the winter at a beach house the way she did."

"She's one of those people who actually like snow. I loved it here when I was a kid."

"What about now?"

"Not sure. I haven't been up here in a while."

"How long you staying?"

On second look, his brown eyes were more amber. I realized he was waiting for an answer and tried to remember the question. "Just until I get another gig."

"How long will that be?"

I shrugged. "Work is sporadic. Especially lately."

"That's one thing I can say about being a bartender. It's steady work. Especially when your boss is your mother."

"I bet. That's why I stopped by. Gypsy said you guys might need someone for a couple of shifts a week."

He straightened up, as if I'd said something wrong. "She didn't say anything to me about hiring someone." He walked to the other end of the bar and began washing glasses in the sink.

I wondered if I'd offended him somehow. After a few minutes, he spoke. "You have experience?"

"Plenty."

He paused. "As a bartender?"

"Yeah, that too. Hotel Elegance in Laguna Beach. I can give you the owner's number if you'd like to call him. He'll probably tell you about my sassy personality. I consider it one of my best traits, but other people don't always agree."

"What would he say about your ability to mix drinks? That is what the job entails, you know."

"He'll tell you I'm one of the best bartenders he's ever had, and if you have time, he might tell you about how I caught the guy who tried to poison his sister."

"We don't have many poisonings here," he deadpanned.

"You never know."

The jazz combo started up and it was too loud to talk, so I just sipped my drink and enjoyed the music. I left before the end of the set to avoid any Luke and Jenna drama. It would have been nice if he'd mentioned that they were dating. Not that I cared.

Chapter Thirteen

I rolled over to turn my phone alarm off, nearly knocking Kit out of bed. "Sorry, girl." She gave me what appeared to be a scolding look, then burrowed under the covers.

After a quick shower, a swipe or two of mascara, and a dab of lip gloss, I headed for the running path where I'd run with Luke before. I brought a small, portable tripod along to take some shots that would hopefully resuscitate my social media presence. Part of me hoped to see Luke, but I only passed two cyclists and a young couple out for an early morning stroll. They held hands and looked at each other longingly, and I had a strong urge to puke.

Relationships always started that way, and people acted as if they wouldn't change, but a year later she'd be yelling at him for leaving his dirty socks on the floor and he'd be making thinly veiled hints that she's getting fat.

I knew there were exceptions, like my grandparents. My grandfather liked being called Gramps, and he teased

Bobbie gently when she refused to be called Grandma, Gran, or even Gigi. They seemed happy and content until Gramps went and had a heart attack.

Gramps left her well off, which helped, no doubt. He came from old money, and she came from no money, and it kept her grounded. Unlike my parents, who seemed to think if other people didn't have money then they should show more initiative and work harder.

I set the tripod on a rock before trying some poses, feeling like an idiot. Once I switched the phone to video things went better, since doing flips and tricks was more in my comfort zone. Plus, it wasn't nearly as embarrassing if someone happened to pass by.

When I returned to the house, I found a freshly brewed pot of coffee, a cat peeking out from under the sofa, and a dog who seemed way too happy to see me.

"You're going to hurt yourself if you're not careful," I scolded as Kit jumped two feet in the air like a miniature kangaroo. I heard loud music coming from my grandmother's bedroom, accompanied by her attempts to hit the high notes. When had she become a fan of Queen?

Kit followed me out to the deck, curling up on my lap as soon as I got settled. I pulled out my phone and reviewed the videos to see which ones I should post. It wasn't easy doing this by myself, but no one had volunteered to follow me around and be my videographer.

Kit's ears came to attention at the sound of the sliding glass door opening. Her tail beat against my thigh.

"Oh, good, you're back." Bobbie carried her coffee cup over to her favorite chair. "I didn't hear you come in. I was meditating. I decided to try chanting today."

"You call singing along to Bohemian Rhapsody chanting?"

She chuckled, pretending I hadn't caught her in a lie. "I do have some good news. Rosa's doctor says she can play if she wears a brace."

"I hope she hasn't told anyone else," I said.

Bobbie raised her eyebrows. "Why?"

"If the groups are being sabotaged, then the Ukulele Ladies should be safe if everyone thinks you have only three members. You can't compete."

The realization hit her. "So, you think someone's trying to sabotage the competition too."

"I don't know." I hated to admit it. "It seems extreme, but we have to admit it's a possibility. I'm wondering about the rule about the group size. Is it new?"

She shook her head. "Any changes to the rules must be voted on. It might be an old rule that hasn't been enforced in years. They post the rules in the newspaper, but they take up two pages, and with all the gobbledygook, I doubt that anyone bothers to read them all the way through."

"If that's the case, I wonder why Alice decided they should start enforcing the rule now?"

Bobbie gave me a thoughtful look. "We'll have to ask her."

She called Rosa, suggesting they keep her improved condition a secret. After discussing several other subjects, she hung up the phone and filled me in on Rosa's side of the conversation.

"She agreed to keep quiet and not let on that she'd be able to play in the competition," Bobbie said.

"We need to figure out who might want to sabotage

the competitors. What I don't understand is why not target the top contenders? Which groups are most likely to win? Wait, let me get something to write with." I put Kit on the ground and went into the kitchen for a notepad and pen.

When I returned, Kit was settled on Bobbie's lap and opened one eye, as if taunting me. I asked Bobbie to list the groups, starting with the ones who had the best chance of winning.

"I'd put my money on The Soul Sisters." She scratched Kit behind one ear, and the dog rolled over on her back, nearly falling off the chair. "Maybe that's why someone put the snake in Vanessa's bathtub."

I wrote the group at the top of my list. "Who's your next choice?"

"The Acapella Fellas," she said.

"People in this town love their puns and rhymes, don't they?"

She gave me a questioning glance. "Do you think so? I'd never noticed."

How could she not have noticed? We could talk about that later. "How many in the Acapella Fellas?"

"Let's see." She paused, counting on her fingers. "I think there are nine or ten of them."

"If someone wanted to disqualify them, they'd have to get rid of five or six of them," I said. "That should mean they're safe."

Bobbie's eyes narrowed ominously. "Unless someone sets off a bomb at one of their rehearsals."

I dropped my pen. We didn't know how far the saboteur would go, and I didn't want people getting hurt because we underestimated him. Or her. "Call them. Tell them not to meet in groups until the police find out who's responsible."

"The police? We're more likely to get to the bottom of this than they are. Bernard told me they still consider Martha's death accidental."

"The Acapella Fellas don't need to know that." I reached for the pen, which had rolled under my chair, but Kit jumped down and grabbed it before I could get it. "In fact, the fewer people who know we're looking into this, the better."

Bobbie called one of the fellas while I chased Kit around the deck. She seemed to think it was a fun game, until I yelled, "Drop it!" The pen fell from her mouth, and she scurried under Bobbie's chair.

"You frightened her," Bobbie scolded.

"Yeah, but I got my pen back." I checked under the chair, only to see Kit's big brown eyes staring back at me. "Sorry, girl. I didn't mean to scare you." I held out my hand and she slowly emerged, allowing me to scratch her behind her ears. "I'm used to big dogs that you can yell at."

"Who knows what sort of life she had before she was rescued," Bobbie said. "She might have been abused."

My heart nearly stopped beating. "Who would... who could?" I scooped the little dog into my arms and held her close to my chest. She rewarded me with an ear lick.

We finished the list, with the Cougar Choir as third most likely to win, followed by the Ukulele Ladies and the Tuba Boys. The Cougar Choir had lost two members since the previous year, leaving them with three members.

"They'll be disqualified unless they find someone to join their group soon," I pointed out.

"I don't think they knew you had to have four members to compete," Bobbie said. "I wonder if any of us did."

I heard a banging. "Is someone knocking on the front door?" I asked.

"It's just Nancy. No need to get up. She knocks to let me know she's coming in, so I'm not startled."

Sure enough, Nancy stuck her head out of the sliding glass door. "Good morning," she said cheerfully.

"You're in a good mood," Bobbie said.

"I was just invited to audition for the Cougar Choir," she said, grinning ear to ear. "I wanted to join last year after Sheila left town, but they had decided to perform as a trio. I guess they just found out that trios can't compete, so they're looking for a new member."

"Yes," Bobbie said. "We all found out at the meeting yesterday."

"Oh." Nancy's face fell. "The Ukulele Ladies only have three now too. Would you like me to wait before I accept an offer from them?"

"Not at all," Bobbie said. "Rosa's wrist isn't broken after all, so we'll be able to compete. Please don't mention it to anyone else."

"And if you do join the Cougar Choir," I added, "I suggest you and the group keep the information to yourselves."

Nancy's eyes widened. "Why is that?"

I stood to stretch my legs. "We think someone might be trying to sabotage some of the competitors."

Nancy gasped. "Do you really think so?"

"Bobbie can fill you in," I said. "Excuse me, but I've got some things to do inside."

I went into my room and lay on the bed. The only thing I had to do was figure out who killed Martha and staged the other accidents, and I hoped a few moments of quiet would help me put the pieces together. Bobbie found Sheila's leaving town suspicious, and without Sheila, the Cougar Choir would have too few members to compete. Did that have something to do with the fact she'd gone missing?

I worried about my grandmother. If someone was targeting the Ukulele Ladies and they learned that Rosa was able to play, then she might be in danger, along with the rest in the group.

A knock on my bedroom door woke me. I glanced at my phone—I'd slept for two hours. I should know better than to lay down in the middle of the day.

"What?" I called out. I knew I sounded rude, but that was my personality the first hour after waking. After that, it improved slightly.

Bobbie opened the door a crack. "I found out the Tuba Boys are rehearsing. I thought we could go talk to them. We can stop by and see Alice afterwards."

My groggy mind tried to make sense of the sentence I'd just heard. "Tuba Boys?" It sounded vaguely familiar.

"They play at the community center, so the sound doesn't disturb half the town." She eyed me accusingly. "Are you taking a nap?"

"Not intentionally," I said. "I wanted to give the little grey cells, as you used to say, a chance to figure things out."

"It was Hercule Poirot who said that."

"Whatever." I sat up on the bed and looked around. "One of my boots is missing."

"I think I saw it under the ottoman in the living room," she said, as if that was perfectly normal.

"Huh?" I might leave my shoes in odd places, but at least I kept them in the same room.

"I think Kit has a fondness for shoes."

I sighed, picked up my boot, and went off in search of the other. "If there are bite marks on my shoes..." I didn't complete the threat, not having the slightest idea how I would exact revenge on a tiny dog.

Under the ottoman, I found my boot, a slipper, three pens, a marker, and the TV remote.

"How did she manage to carry my boot into the living room? I think it weighs more than she does." I sat down and pulled on my boots before she could run off with them again.

"Never judge by appearances," Bobbie said.

I glanced at her flowing tunic and beaded necklaces. She had a point. Anyone who didn't know her would think she was a dotty old lady, but that was far from the truth. "We need to stop at the pet store on the way back and get Kit something to chew on," I said.

"The pet store? It's a hundred miles to the nearest one."

"Okay, the General Store then. If nothing else, I can buy her a case of cheap pens." Bobbie gave me a look as if I were the worst person ever. "Is that a bad idea? I never said I was a dog expert."

Kit came over to me, rubbed against my feet, and

flopped on her back, a less than subtle hint that she wanted belly rubs. Or she was trying to charm me out of my shoes. I reached down and gave her a quick pet, and when I stood, she jumped up, anticipating my next move.

Before I reached the door, Kit had her nose pressed up against the door jamb. "Sorry, Kit. You can't come with us."

"Why not?" Bobbie asked.

"Not you too," I said. "It's a conspiracy. Kit can't go with us everywhere. Like restaurants."

I stepped outside into a dismal scene. A thick layer of grey clouds obscured the sun. I could have been sitting on the patio at my parents' beach house if Bobbie hadn't insisted on coming home just in time for the cold and wet weather of late fall. My masochistic streak insisted I check my phone for the weather in Laguna Beach. Seventy-two degrees. Here in Arrow Springs, we'd be lucky if it hit fifty. I reached in my jacket pocket for my knit hat and pulled it on.

We arrived at the community center just as the Tuba Boys were packing up for a lunch break. Among the cases leaned up against the wall, only one appeared tuba sized.

Bobbie noticed, too. "How can you be the Tuba Boys with only one tuba?" she asked the group.

"We're not the Tuba Boys anymore," the older man I'd seen earlier said. And when I say older, I mean as close to the grave as you can be while still walking under your own power. He reached out a hand to me. "I'm George."

I shook his hand then forgot all about George and the rest of the Tuba Boys. Luke, looking casually handsome in a pullover sweater and jeans, bent over an instrument case.

Before I pulled my hat off, I remembered the cold-weather hazard—hat hair—and left it on. I might look like a dork, but hoped my rosy cheeks made up for it.

"What are you doing here?" I asked Luke. "Don't tell me you play the saxophone *and* the tuba."

Luke gave me a warm smile. "Hi, Whit. I play the French horn."

"So, the Tuba Boys needed a French horn player?"

George cut into what I considered our private conversation. "We've reformed as a brass quintet. Kiss My Brass."

"What did you just say?" I looked from George to Luke.

Luke started laughing. "Don't look at me. I didn't come up with the name."

"We were never going to win as a tuba group," George explained. "So, two of us traded in our tubas for trumpets and one switched to trombone. Then, all we had to do was convince Luke to join us. I think we're a shoo-in this year."

I glanced at Bobbie who raised her eyebrows to let me know she had the same thought as me.

"Especially when the Soul Sisters are disqualified," I said.

"And the Ukulele Ladies," Bobbie added.

"What are you talking about?" George asked.

Bobbie explained to George, Luke, and the other members of Kiss My Brass about the four-person requirement for the competition.

"Forgive me for saying so," George said. "But the only competition we're worried about is the Blarney Band."

"Blarney Band?" I hadn't heard about them before.

"They play Irish music, mostly traditional tunes."

Luke said. "It's their first time in the competition, but they could win. I went to school with their fiddle player."

"I went and spied on one of their rehearsals. They're really good," George said. "Don't get me wrong, we're competitive, but I'd rather win because we're the best, not because someone was disqualified."

"Yeah, I'm sorry to break it to you," Luke said, "but if someone is attacking the Ukulele Ladies, it's not because they're worried about the competition."

Bobbie appeared deflated. "Thank you for the information. I'll let you go have your lunch now."

As we walked away, I asked. "What about me? Can we have our lunch now?"

"Let's stop by and see Alice first."

❦ ⇢

A short walk took us to City Hall. I followed Bobbie down a wide corridor to the mayor's office, where we found Alice eating a sandwich at her desk.

Bobbie greeted her. "I hope we're not interrupting your lunch."

Alice wiped her mouth on a napkin and smiled, seemingly glad to have visitors. "Hello, Bobbie. How nice to see you." She found a spiral bound book under some papers and flipped through the pages. "Do you have an appointment with the mayor?"

"We came to see you," Bobbie said.

"Me?" Alice's face lit up, and she looked at the two of us expectantly.

I felt bad that we only came to grill her about the

competition rules, but I should have known that Bobbie would be able to finesse the situation.

"I hoped to get your opinion, since you have so much experience with music and the competition," Bobbie said. "You know, the Ukulele Ladies are down to three members."

Alice's smile slipped away. "I never told you how sorry I was about Martha. You must be heartbroken. Such a nice lady."

I thought about what people might say if I died suddenly, and I didn't think "nice lady" would be in my eulogy.

"She was," Bobbie agreed. "And with her gone, and Rosa's wrist injured, Gypsy, Ralph, and I aren't sure if we want to continue with the competition. I mean, we'd need to find another ukulele player, but that's not really the issue. It's just so sad, you know?"

"I understand exactly what you're saying. But don't you think Martha would want you to compete? She loved being a Ukulele Lady."

Bobbie appeared to think this over. "I hadn't thought of it that way." She turned to me. "What do you think?"

I gave them what I hoped was a warm smile, using long dormant muscles. "I think Alice is right. Too bad about the rule change. It's short notice to break in a new member."

Alice's eyes widened. "There wasn't a rule change. From the beginning of the competition, there was a size requirement. It makes it fairer. How would you feel if an amazing soloist moved to town and decided to enter? Or a big band or an orchestra?"

Bobbie nodded as if considering the idea. "But it's never been enforced, at least not as long as I can remember. What changed this year?"

"A concerned citizen stopped by. She had read all the rules—I haven't even read them all in at least a decade—and she felt it was important for everyone to know ahead of time. Otherwise, several groups could be disqualified at the last minute when it was too late to recruit new members."

"That would have sucked if you'd found out right before the competition," I told Bobbie.

"What would our little town do without our concerned citizens?" Bobbie asked, her smile as sweet as syrup. "Who suggested you remind the participants of the rule? I'd like to thank them for being so thoughtful."

I thought she laid it on thick, but even so, Alice wasn't biting.

"I promised not to mention it to anyone," she said. "And I never break a promise."

Chapter Fourteen

We stopped in at the General Store, which I'd heard had a surprisingly good deli counter. While Bobbie ordered sandwiches, I walked the aisles looking for something for Kit to chew on other than my shoes. I slowed down as I passed by multi packs of cheap pens, briefly considering buying them. Bobbie might not get the joke, so I kept looking until I found the pet section and a bag of rawhide chews.

As I pulled out of the General Store parking lot, Bobbie told me to turn right instead of left, the opposite of the way home.

"Okay, where are we going now?"

"Just drive."

I eyed the bag with our sandwiches hungrily, but complied. Maybe she knew a good picnic place. Personally, I thought our deck would be the ideal spot for lunch, and besides, we hadn't bought drinks.

After turning down one winding road after another, I

drove up a steep driveway to an enormous split-level house surrounded by tall pine trees.

"Nice house," I said. "Who are we visiting? I'm not giving them my sandwich. Charity begins at home, in case you haven't heard."

"You can stay here and eat your sandwich if you'd like. I'm going to check things out."

I reached for the bag, pulling out what was sure to be a delicious turkey and provolone sub. "Check what things out?"

"This is Sheila's house." She stepped out of the car, leaving me to decide between lunch and keeping her out of trouble. I took a big bite of the sandwich before reluctantly following her to the front door. Dead pine needles covered the walkway and I nearly tripped over a pinecone.

She rang the bell, waited, then knocked.

"Who lives here now?" I stood at the front door while Bobbie bent over, searching through the shrubbery. "What are you doing?"

She straightened up with a groan, brandishing a key proudly. "I just knocked to make sure no one was here." She unlocked the front door and stepped inside.

"I think this is a bad idea." I considered going back to the car and my sandwich, but curiosity got the better of me and I followed her into the living room. We entered a cavernous redwood-paneled room with vaulted ceilings, and Bobbie searched the house while I waited in the living room, admiring the view of the canyon through floor to ceiling windows.

I wandered into a spacious, modern kitchen where everything seemed in place—no dishes in the drainer to offend the dish police. I eyed the expanse of counter space with envy. I might not cook, but I could appreciate fine granite. I opened the refrigerator door. "Ugh."

Bobbie had just returned from searching the other rooms. "What did you find?"

"Grossness. Why didn't she clean out her refrigerator before she left town?" Even I knew better than to leave produce behind for more than a few days.

Bobbie frowned. "Her underwear drawer is empty."

I closed the refrigerator door. "That at least makes sense."

"Does it?" She put her hands on her hips. "Do you take all your underwear when you travel?"

"All except for the old ones with the stretched-out elastic or the ones that don't fit quite right. I bought some thongs a while back, but I hate the way they creep up my butt. I can't bring myself to throw them away."

"TMI," she said, shaking her head. "Everyone has panties they can't bring themselves to throw away, but they don't bring them along on vacation."

"I think the rotten veggies in the fridge are a bigger clue," I said, as if it were a competition.

"Look what I found in a bedside table." She held up a well-worn address book. "Sheila texted her friends that she'd gone to visit her daughter. I bet the daughter's number is in here."

"Great." I was getting antsy, hanging out in someone's home without their permission. "Are we done here?"

"As soon as I go through her office."

I followed her into a room that appeared to be a catch-all—like a room-sized junk drawer. A treadmill sat in one corner next to an oversized chair and a sewing machine. A big-screen TV hung on the opposite wall. Bobbie went straight to the desk and started digging through drawers.

"Aha," she said as she held up a checkbook. I remembered my father showing me one once when I was a teenager, explaining how to balance an account. That was two hours of my life I'd never get back. Bobbie flipped through the checkbook's register.

"What are you looking for?" My discomfort at her invading Sheila's privacy was balanced by my curiosity.

"I'll know when I see it." She stopped at a page. "Well, that's interesting."

She showed me an entry showing a two-thousand-dollar check dated three months prior with Luke as the payee. She reviewed more entries and found another check written to Luke for four thousand around the time she reportedly left town.

"Why would Sheila be giving Luke that kind of money?" Bobbie asked me, as if I had some special insider knowledge.

"Maybe he was helping her with…" I paused, trying to think of an answer that didn't make him look bad. "Yeah, I got nothing." I'd have to find out if he did handyman work on the side.

We locked up, and I headed for the car, while Bobbie walked over to the overstuffed mailbox. After flipping through a stack of envelopes, she got into the passenger side.

"Shall I add tampering with federal mail to your list of crimes?" Two crimes in one day seemed a lot for someone who rarely got a parking ticket.

"I put the mail back," she said defensively. "There were a couple of envelopes with pink showing through the windows." When I gave her a quizzical look, she explained, "That means the bills are late. Those are usually the final notice before they turn off your utilities."

"People still get bills in the mail?"

"Yes. Now let's get out of here before someone calls the cops." She didn't have to tell me twice.

The temperature had warmed several degrees, but by the time we reached home a steady drizzle began to fall. Hat hair and frizz—what a great combo.

Bobbie made a pot of coffee, which always meant she meant business. I joined her at the kitchen table while she searched Sheila's address book for her daughter's number.

"Maybe she has a different last name," I suggested. "Or maybe Sheila has the number memorized or programmed in her phone and didn't feel the need to write it down."

Bobbie seemed to accept my explanation begrudgingly. She went through the entries, looking for names she didn't recognize.

"How old is Sheila?"

Bobbie, focused on her task, didn't look up. "She looks around fifty, but I'm sure she's older, maybe sixty or so. She worked hard to look young." She seemed to sense my misgivings. "She liked to have flings with younger men, and I'm sure she went after Luke. That doesn't mean he took her up on her offer."

"Offer?" If that meant sex, I doubted that many young men would turn down an attractive, experienced woman's advances, especially if there were no strings attached.

Besides, it might explain the checks. Who knew being a gigolo paid so well?

We split up the phone numbers and decided to say we'd misplaced her daughter's number and were calling to check on Sheila.

I hung up from my fifth call, striking out again. One number was disconnected, two barely remembered Sheila, one was a friend of her late husband's, and one was a former neighbor from several years earlier who asked me to give Sheila her love when I saw her again.

Bobbie was having a lively discussion with someone and seemed to be updating them on everything that had happened in Arrow Springs for the past decade or two. I leaned over to look at her list.

"Are you still on the first call?" I asked, and when she nodded, I took the rest of the list. If I left it up to Bobbie, we'd be at this all day.

On the last call, I hit pay dirt. The woman was an old friend who'd known Sheila decades earlier in Boise, Idaho, where they'd both raised their families. Their sons had played together as kids.

"Daughter?" she asked in a quizzical tone. "You say she went to stay with her daughter?"

"Yes, that's what she said."

"Well, isn't that something?" I could hear the smile in her voice.

"Why do you say that?"

"They haven't talked in years. Let me think. It must be... fifteen years? Twenty? It broke Sheila's heart. Jocelyn wouldn't even take her phone calls."

"Why not?"

"They had a falling out. Jocelyn didn't approve of her mother's lifestyle after the divorce, from what Sheila told me. How delightful that they're talking again." Her voice trailed off.

"Is something wrong?"

"No," she paused before going on. "Just me being self-ish. I don't know why Sheila didn't call me to tell me the news. Maybe she wanted to wait and see how the visit went first."

"Yes, that must be it." I thanked her and hung up just as Bobbie finished her call. "What did you learn?" I asked.

"Mayor Mishchuk," she began, "not the current one, but his late father, had a love child with a Hollywood star-let. They sent the girl to a convent to be raised by nuns, and no one knows what happened to her."

"In other words, you learned nothing."

"One never knows what information might be useful."

I managed to refrain from rolling my eyes and filled her in on what I'd learned about Sheila's daughter, Jocelyn.

"I knew it. There's no way her daughter just showed up after twenty years unexpectedly without telling anyone. She would have called Sheila before coming to visit, and Sheila would have told everyone. At least her friends."

"Well..." I had to admit, it was starting to seem a bit fishy. "Maybe."

She gave me a tight-lipped smirk. "Do you expect me to believe that Jocelyn swooped into town, picked up Sheila and all her underwear, and didn't let her tell her friends?"

"When you put it that way, it does seem unlikely." I hated to jump to conclusions, but I didn't have an alternate explanation for Sheila suddenly leaving town.

"I think tomorrow I'll do a neighborhood."

"You might want to rephrase that," I suggested. "If someone overheard you, it could ruin your reputation."

"What reputation?" She gave me a wink. "Doing a neighborhood or a neighborhood investigation is what we PIs call going door to door, asking people what they saw. They may have seen something or someone around Martha's house the night she died and not realize its importance."

I'd heard worse ideas.

I woke before dawn, even though I didn't need to be in L.A. until three that afternoon. I had a good feeling about the meeting with Madison, and I was more than a little curious about why Kyle wanted to meet.

With time to kill, I put on running clothes, hoping a run would help dissipate some of my nervous energy. I'd nearly reached the river when I heard a bark behind me. That darn dog had gotten out again.

"I'm not slowing down for you, so you better keep up." When we reached the river road, she turned in the wrong direction, toward the rockslide Luke had told me about. "Stop!" I yelled, but that seemed to make her run faster.

"Darn it." I chased after her, wondering if dog-chasing was going to be a regular thing from now on. She reached the rockslide ahead of me, jumping up on the rocks and leaping from boulder to boulder like a mountain goat. I yelled for her to stop, but after a quick look over her shoulder at me, she kept going.

She showed no fear, but then, she didn't risk an ankle sprain by climbing over the uneven surfaces. I'd nearly caught up with her when she reached the other side of the slide and took off again.

"Get back here!" I chased after her full speed now, nearly catching up when she stopped and put her nose up, smelling the air. A moment later, she turned sharply, running along the river.

She stopped at the muddy bank, digging and barking her fool head off. I approached slowly, trying to catch my breath and hoping she wouldn't run off again. She stopped digging and sat still, wagging her once-fluffy tail in the muck. She'd need another bath once I got her home, which might be the perfect way to punish her for running off.

All thoughts of punishments and baths evaporated when I looked at what she'd uncovered. It appeared to be the remains of some animal. My wishful thinking evaporated when I took a closer look. Animals didn't wear nail polish.

Chapter Fifteen

I turned away from the sight, feeling lightheaded. The body had been there a while, but I still felt an urgency to get help. Or maybe I just didn't want to be alone with a dead body.

I grabbed Kit, clutching the dog to my chest while I tried to get a signal on my phone. At first, she wriggled to get down, but soon calmed down and rested her head on my chest. The phone stubbornly stayed at one bar and any attempt at a phone call or text failed. I nearly gave up and went home, but I didn't want to leave the crime scene, assuming that's what it was. Who was I kidding? No one accidentally buried themselves.

Climbing on top of a nearby pile of boulders, I finally managed a staticky call. After repeating myself three times, and not being at all sure I was understood or believed, the operator informed me the police were on their way. I found a relatively flat rock to sit on and stared unseeing at the trickling river.

Due to the inaccessibility of the area, I knew we were in for a long wait. I held Kit in my lap, and she laid her head on my now-muddy knees, as if she were waiting too.

The police arrived, followed by paramedics and crime scene personnel. As soon as I answered their questions and gave them my contact information, the officer in charge allowed me to leave. Bobbie would be worried if she had noticed how long we'd been gone. I walked back, holding Kit tightly to make sure she didn't take off again.

The moment I opened the door, Bobbie started in on me. "Where have you two been? You need to let me know when you're going to be gone that long. I've been worried sick." Kit jumped up on her legs, brushing mud all over her pants. Bobbie looked from the muddy dog to me. "What have you two gotten into?"

"I think you'll want to sit down," I said, heading for the liquor cabinet. She'd want a drink once she heard what I had to tell her. I knew I wanted one.

"I don't need to sit down to listen to—" She stopped speaking when she saw the look on my face. "What's happened? Are you okay?"

"I think we found Sheila." It was a guess, but my gut told me that's whose body Kit had found.

Her face transformed from concerned to hopeful, but the smile froze on her face as she realized we hadn't found her alive. She took a few steps back and collapsed onto the sofa. I poured us each a glass of sherry and told her what I knew.

"I need to take a shower and get ready to drive to L.A." I hated leaving her alone, but this meeting might resuscitate my career.

Was I crazy? I'd just found a dead body and my grandmother might be in danger. "Never mind. I should stay."

"No, go. I'll be fine."

"Do you want me to call someone to come over and be with you?"

"What?" She blinked, struggling to focus on my words. "You know what this means, don't you?"

It meant a lot of things, including that there really was a murderer in Arrow Springs. "What?"

"The police will have to take it seriously now."

"It also means that someone has murdered two old... um, mature women. Women you knew. I don't think you're safe—you or your friends."

Her face went slack as the realization hit home. "You really think so?"

"Sheila and Martha have, or had, nothing in common besides participating in the competition, and we've pretty much ruled that out as a motive." The meeting in L.A. might get me my career out of the dumpster, but Bobbie was more important. "That's it. I'm staying."

"I'll call Rosa and Gypsy and have them over. They shouldn't be alone either." Bobbie looked at her muddy pants and stood. "After I change my pants. They can help me find out what else Martha and Sheila had in common, like friends or other hobbies."

"No poking around until I get back, okay? It might be dangerous if someone thought you were getting too close to the truth."

She didn't answer. She didn't make eye contact.

No way was I going anywhere if I couldn't trust her to stay out of trouble. "I'll call and cancel my meeting."

"No, no." She gave me a sheepish look. "I'll be good."

Chapter Sixteen

I t was late morning by the time I headed down the curvy mountain roads, taking the curves as fast as I wanted. Whenever Bobbie was in the car, she clutched her armrest and gasped when the tires squealed, which took all the fun out of it. I hit the 91 freeway and set the cruise control, which allowed me to let my thoughts wander.

If anything happened to Bobbie, what would I do? She'd been the one steady person in my life—the one person who didn't need to say out loud they loved you. You just knew it.

Thinking about the possibility of losing Bobbie didn't seem like the way to prepare for an important meeting. I couldn't do anything about keeping her safe from my car, so I turned the radio up and sang along off key. Loud.

Arriving at Bob's Big Boy in Burbank, I pulled into the parking lot with ten minutes to spare. From the outside, Bob's looked just the way it did when I was a kid. My parents would never patronize such a commonplace restaurant, but a friend's parents took us several times.

The inside hadn't changed either. Burnt orange booths lined the walls, and lunch patrons crowded the long counter. The space-age inspired light fixtures were so dated they'd come back in style.

I spotted Madison at a booth halfway back and headed her way. A man sat across from her with his back to me. She introduced me to the stunt coordinator. As soon as I shook his hand, I could see in his eyes that it wasn't going to happen. We went through the motions anyway.

I ordered a Big Boy hamburger—a double decker with cheese with a side of fries. We chatted while we ate, talking about people we knew and shows we'd worked on. He asked me a few questions about my experience and the types of stunts I could do, which was all of them.

"Whit is a former gymnast," Madison said, trying to be helpful. "She was on the Olympic team as an alternate."

This didn't seem to impress him. He picked up the bill and slid a credit card out of his wallet. "We'll call as soon as we've made the decision."

I looked him in the eye. "Except you won't, will you? I had a very good reason to flip that director onto his back. I'm surprised applause didn't break out when I did it. Everyone knows his reputation for harassing women, but no one does anything about it. Why is everyone so afraid of him?"

He paused and took a deep breath, no doubt deciding how to reply. "Look, maybe if you just apologized to the guy."

I stared at him dumbfounded. The sound in the room

faded away, and I could hear my heart beating. What could I say to something so delusional? Nothing. I slid out of the booth and headed for the door.

Madison followed me into the parking lot. "Whit, wait." When I didn't answer or slow down, she added, "Please."

I stopped and turned to face her, wondering what she could possibly have to say. If she wanted to defend me, she could have done it at the table with the coordinator. "He thinks I should apologize? It's bad enough what women have to put up with in this industry from a few men who can't keep their hands to themselves. But the real problem is people like him who not only let him get away with it, but they expect women to keep quiet and not make waves."

"Just give it some time," she said. "Eventually it will all blow over."

There were so many things I wanted to say, so much I could have said, but I didn't think it would make any difference.

"I don't want it to blow over," I said. "I want things to change. If working in this industry means ignoring people who harass and use us because they're in positions of power, I'm not sure I want to be a part of it."

She slowly nodded, as if silently agreeing. "I wish I could afford to have your attitude, but I need to work." Her voice was quiet and full of regret. "Take care of yourself, Whit."

I got into my car but didn't start it right away, taking a minute to calm down and think about what had just happened. Was my career over?

If I wasn't a stunt performer, what was I? What other marketable skills did I have? I doubted if anyone would pay me to make snarky quips or compose sassy comebacks. Go to work for an amusement park in one of their stunt shows? There were worse jobs, but still I hoped it didn't come to that.

Bartending kept me busy and put a few dollars in the bank, but it wasn't a career, at least not for me. I could always teach gymnastics, but I had hoped to save that option for retirement when I was too old for stunt work.

I sat up straight and pulled my shoulders back. I wasn't a quitter, and besides, I loved stunt work. I would figure out a way to revive my career, whatever it took.

In half an hour, I was meeting Kyle for a drink. I considered bailing on him and heading back to Arrow Springs, but then I'd have to wonder why Kyle wanted to meet. This day couldn't get any worse, so I pulled up the directions to the restaurant on my phone.

I arrived at the trendy eatery early, which gave me time to freshen up in the restroom. I found a seat at a tall table in the lounge and waited.

I looked up just as Kyle entered the restaurant. In a city full of handsome actors and models, he stood out. Sure, he was good looking—tall with dark hair and grey eyes—but there was something about the way he carried himself. He exuded confidence.

I caught his eye, and he headed my way, wearing a shy smile. That smile had hooked me when I first met him in taekwondo class. In reality, he wasn't the least bit shy.

He gave me a kiss on the cheek. "Hey, girl," he said casually. "You look great. The mountain air is doing you good." The blonde server, who had ignored me until now, rushed over to take our order.

We made small talk while waiting for our drinks. He asked me about my parents and my grandmother, and I decided not to tell him about the two dead women. Something like that might put a damper on the conversation. I impatiently waited to find out what he had to say.

The server put our drinks down, and turned to Kyle, giving her hair a flirtatious flip. "Would you like anything else?"

He gave her one of his famous smiles. "I think that's all for now."

"Are you..." she began. "I hope you don't mind me asking, but I watched Law and Order last night, and I wondered..."

He shrugged modestly. "Yeah, that was me."

"I knew it!" she said, as if she'd answered an especially obscure Jeopardy question. "You were really great."

"We'll let you know if we need anything else," I said.

She shot me a glare, but at least she left.

Kyle took a sip of his martini and cleared his throat. "I'm glad we were able to get together. I have something I wanted to tell you."

His serious demeanor made me suspect he wasn't about to beg me to take him back. I waited for him to continue.

"I'm getting married," he said.

"What?" That was one of the last things I expected him to say. I could feel annoyance rising through my body, tightening my shoulders. "Who is it?"

He smiled, and I felt my annoyance begin to morph into rage. "It's Madison."

"Madison?" I heard my voice rise, and I tried to control my temper. "Madison the stuntwoman?" I felt my phone vibrate in my pocket. "The one I introduced you to?"

"Yeah," he admitted, attempting to appear contrite, but failing.

"I just had lunch with her and that douche-bag stunt coordinator." I watched his face which showed no surprise. "Did you know about that?"

"I kinda suggested it," he said. "Everyone knows you're one of the best in the business. I wanted to know why you weren't working."

My phone buzzed again. I pulled it out of my pocket to see who was calling. Bobbie. I considered letting it go to voicemail, but I figured I could use a break from my drama with Kyle.

"Hi, Bobbie."

"I've been thinking," she said.

"Um, that's good." I made a half-hearted attempt to hide my irritation. "Thanks for letting me know."

She sighed loudly. "What if Nancy killed Martha and caused Rosa's accident? She wanted to be a Ukulele Lady so badly, she started getting rid of members thinking we'd ask her to join. Maybe she didn't mean for Martha to die, she just wanted her out of commission for a few weeks. I bet you anything she's the one who went to Alice to get her to enforce the rules."

This made surprising sense. Crap. And we'd told Nancy that Rosa would be able to play after all. We'd kept it a secret from everyone except the one person who should have been kept in the dark.

"I'm on my way." I jumped off my stool. "I should be there in two or three hours. Lock all the doors and don't go out. Promise?"

After a long moment of silence, I heard her reply. "I promise."

I hung up and jumped off my stool. "By the way, Kyle, telling your ex that you're getting married is just the sort of thing that text messaging is perfect for." I took one step toward the door, but I had one more thing I wanted to say to him. "Screw you."

I wanted to say more, but I'd promised Bobbie I'd clean up my language.

On the way back to Arrow Springs, my frustration built as the traffic slowed. When I finally arrived home and found Bobbie safe and sound, I let myself breathe again.

She met me at the door, coat and purse in hand as if she'd been waiting all afternoon for me. I grabbed her in a hug and held on tight until I heard her muffled voice.

"Air, please?"

I let her go and she straightened her blouse, brushing out imaginary wrinkles. She didn't try to hide her smile.

"Will you take me over to Mr. Fernsby's office? I'd like to get an update on Martha's and Sheila's cases."

"Sure." I wouldn't mind more tacos now that my appetite had returned.

Ten minutes later, we sat in his office, and I told him about finding Sheila's body that morning. It felt like something that had happened weeks ago.

Bernard leaned back in his chair, his chins resting on his chest. "Yes, I heard from one of my friends on the force. I informed my client, so that case is closed. Not the way I would have liked it to end."

Bobbie slapped the table, causing him to jerk upright, now completely alert. "I want you to reopen the case and solve her murder. I think it's connected to Martha's death."

"I'd be very surprised if it isn't." Bernard leaned forward, his elbows on his desk. "Two suspicious deaths in a small town like ours is too many to be coincidental."

"What updates do you have on Martha?"

Bernard opened the file in front of him and shared the police report with us. "No sign of forced entry," he read.

"That means it's someone she knew," Bobbie said. "Someone she would have let in her house, or someone—"

"Not necessarily," I said. "Remember the key hidden in the shrubbery?"

"Oh, right." Bobbie slumped back in her chair, her expression gloomy.

Stupid keys. "I hope you don't have a key hidden outside your house." The look on her face told me she did. "When we get home—"

She held up a hand, cutting me off. "We'll talk about that later. Let Mr. Fernsby continue."

Bernard explained the toxicology report would take another week or so, but everything else pointed to heart failure brought about by the electrocution. "The police are treating it as an accident."

"Of course they are," Bobbie groused. "No reason to make extra work for themselves."

He nodded, seeming to concur. "I'd be inclined to agree with them except for one thing."

"What is that?" I asked.

Bernard took a picture out of the file. "I managed to get copies of the crime scene photos. On close inspection, I caught a detail the report doesn't mention. The person responsible did their best to make it appear as if the wire that fell into the puddle had been chewed by rats or other vermin, but see here?" He handed Bobbie a magnifying glass and pointed to a spot on the picture. "There's clearly a clean cut through the insulation on this side of the wire."

"You're right," Bobbie said, looking up at him with admiration. "Good catch."

"I may look like a washed-up old PI, but I've still got my marbles. And a lot more experience than our current police force."

I reached for the photo for a closer look. That settled it. "And then there's the breaker."

Bernard raised his eyebrows. "What breaker?"

"One of the breakers was flipped off." I pulled out my phone and showed him the picture I'd taken the night we'd found Martha in her basement. "Someone did that to lure Martha into the basement. The power went off somewhere in the house, and she had to step in the puddle of water to turn it back on."

"Good work," Bernard said. "I think I'm going to like having you work for me."

I pointed at Bobbie. "She's the one helping. I'm just here for the tacos."

Bobbie waited in the car while I ordered tacos with extra guacamole. She didn't talk on the short drive, possibly thinking about what Bernard had said. As soon as we arrived home, I insisted she take the spare key out from under the rock where she'd hidden it. "Monday, I'm calling and getting the locks changed."

Bobbie didn't respond.

"One, two, or three tacos?" I asked cheerfully, hoping to distract her from thoughts of death.

"I'm not hungry." Her listless manner disturbed me. This wasn't the plucky grandmother I knew.

"I'll make you waffles."

We sat at the dining room table while I gobbled down tacos and she stared at her plate.

"More syrup?" I asked. Bobbie had only taken a bite or two of her waffles even though they were blueberry, her favorite.

"I think I'll go to bed early." She carried her dishes into the kitchen and said goodnight.

I hadn't been to bed by eight o'clock since I'd been a child, and I wasn't about to start now. I poured a glass of wine and plopped on the sofa with one of Bobbie's cookbooks. Not that I hoped to learn any cooking techniques, but the pictures were fun to look at. Besides, whenever I got stuck on a problem, I often found that an unrelated and relatively mindless task would jog my brain. Sometimes, an answer would come seemingly out of nowhere.

I didn't get past page five. Around midnight, I woke with a stiff neck and crawled off to bed.

Chapter Seventeen

The next morning, I found Bobbie humming in the kitchen, which made me happy. She informed me that when she'd finished breakfast, she would be walking to Rosa's house. Ralph and Gypsy were joining them for a top-secret rehearsal.

"Oh no you don't," I said. "I'm driving you."

On the way, Bobbie said, "Don't forget. Kit has an appointment at the vet at ten this morning."

"Huh?" This was the first I'd heard about a vet visit. "When did you make an appointment for her? And why? She seems perfectly healthy to me."

"I'm sure I told you," Bobbie said. "Well, never mind. Angela called and said Kit needs a checkup and rabies shot. Arrow Springs Veterinary Clinic is on Blue Jay Lane, just around the corner from the Community Center."

When I returned from dropping her off, I set a timer on my phone so I wouldn't forget Kit's appointment. Inertia kept me stretched out on the sofa scrolling through emails and social media on my phone with Kit snuggled next to me.

Mr. Whiskers made his way along the top of the sofa toward me and began biting my hair. It didn't hurt, and I figured he'd been through enough, so I did my best to ignore him. When Kit noticed the cat, they locked eyes, and a low growl began to form in her throat.

"Knock it off," I said. She gave one more growl before burrowing under the afghan. I guessed a truce was the best we could hope for.

The timer went off and I went searching for Kit's leash. She jumped up and down until I gave a stern command: "Sit." She cowered at the sound of my voice and a pang of guilt stabbed me.

"Were people mean to you in your previous life?" I asked Kit as I hooked the leash onto her collar. "Don't worry. That's all in the past now. I'll try very, very hard not to yell at you from now on."

She happily wagged her tail which I took as a sign that she'd already forgiven me. Her demeanor changed the moment we walked through the doors of the vet clinic. She trembled as I held her on my lap while we waited.

When her name was called, we stepped into a small room with a metal table. I tried to put her on the table, but she climbed onto me, nearly climbing over my shoulder.

I stroked her fur and spoke softly trying to calm her. "It's okay, girl. I won't let them hurt you." Then I remembered the rabies shot she needed. "I'll be right here for you, okay?"

The veterinarian entered, a dark-haired woman about my age. After introducing herself, she asked several questions. When I told her Kit was a rescue, she asked more questions, including the name of the rescue organization.

"I'm not sure," I said. "My mother got her for me, but she didn't tell me their name."

Did I imagine the suspicious look she gave me? I brushed off the feeling as she brought out a handheld device that she waved around Kit's neck.

"I'm checking for a microchip," she said

"Yeah, my mom said the rescue put one in."

"And there it is," she said as the unit beeped. A moment later, the thing beeped again. She frowned.

"Something wrong?" I asked.

She glanced at me, then back to the device. "It's registering two microchips." She gave me a reassuring smile. "That's not that unusual. If a dog changes hands, we don't remove the previous owner's chip. Not all scanners can pick up every make of chip like this one just did. I'll just record the information for both chips and confirm the information."

"Does that mean you might be able to tell who she belonged to before?" I asked. "She does some really cool tricks, and we wondered who'd trained her." I didn't mention that we'd also wondered why someone would let go of a dog after spending so much time training them.

"Due to privacy regulations, I wouldn't be able to give you the information on a previous owner without their permission." She proceeded to give Kit an exam, offering advice on her diet, grooming, and flea and tick control.

Kit got her shots, and I paid the bill. Her tail wagged faster than a hummingbird's wings as we left.

The clouds had drifted away, leaving the sky a shade

of blue I'd never seen in the city. When we got home, Kit slipped under the sofa, and I guessed I wouldn't see her for several hours as she recovered from her ordeal.

I took my lunch out on the deck to enjoy the fresh air and listen to the soft, rustling sound of the trees in the breeze. I'd gotten used to the slow rhythm of the mountains, and that concerned me. Was I losing my preference for city air full of honking horns and carbon monoxide?

My phone rang and I jumped. Gypsy's number showed on the display.

"It's very last minute," she said, sounding apologetic, "but I wondered if you could work the bar tonight. I have an event to attend, and our server called out sick, so Elijah will have to cover the tables and the bar. It would be a lot easier on him if you could help bartend."

I could sure use the money. "I'd be happy to." I agreed to stop by around five so Elijah could give me the lay of the land.

I'd leaned back in my deck chair hoping to resume my nap when the phone rang again. Twice in one day must be some sort of a record.

"Hi Whit. It's Jenna," the voice said. "I was hoping you had time to talk."

Talk? Why would I want to talk to potentially psycho-stalker Jenna? "I'm kind of busy."

"I'm in front of your house."

I jumped out of my chair and headed for the living room, my heart beating faster. The girl had no boundaries. "What are you doing here?"

I heard her sigh through the phone. "I came to apologize, and then I thought maybe it was rude to just drop in since I wasn't invited." She paused, and when I didn't answer, she added, "I guess I can tell you I'm sorry over the phone. It's just that, well, I guess I have some insecurities about my relationship with Luke. Which isn't really a relationship. I mean, I wanted it to be a relationship, but I guess it was just wishful thinking on my part."

I peeked out the window, making sure she couldn't see me. She stood on the front lawn, a forlorn little girl.

"You need to stop trying so hard," I said. "Give people a little space. No one wants to be smothered."

"You're right. I know you're right, but when you really like someone, and you think maybe they like you... Anyway, sorry to bother you. I'll go now." She hung up the phone and walked toward her car. She turned around at the sound of me opening the front door, a hopeful expression on her face.

"You might as well come in." I hoped I wouldn't regret this.

Kit scooted out from under the sofa to greet her, but ran off when Mr. Whiskers came out from his hiding place.

"Is this...?" Jenna picked up the cat, cradling it in her arms. "It is! Mr. Whiskers!"

I didn't question why she knew Mr. Whiskers, since everyone in this town seemed to know each other. Why wouldn't they know their pets, too?

Holding Mr. Whiskers like a baby, she wandered around the living room, taking in the furnishings, and inspecting the mantel photos. She peered out at the deck. "You have a lovely house."

"It's Bobbie's." I led her to the kitchen breakfast bar. "How about a daiquiri?"

Her eyes lit up. "Like a strawberry daiquiri?"

I did my best to refrain from an eye roll, but sheesh. "No, a real, honest to goodness daiquiri. I'll make you one and if you don't like it, I'll see if we have any white zinfandel." I did my best to accept all kinds of people, no matter their race, creed, sexual orientation, or social status, but I found it tough not to judge anyone who drank white zin.

I filled my shaker with ice and set about squeezing limes, carrying on a conversation while I worked. "How long have you and Luke dated?"

She scrunched her face in a somehow endearing grimace. "We haven't really been on a date. We just hang out together when he plays at Gypsy's. And we go to the gym together three times a week."

"Together?" I asked.

"Well, not together, but we sort of meet there."

"Uh, huh. So, you guys hang out." That sounded like typical relationship behavior for anyone under thirty. Dinner and a movie were so 2005. Adding the rum and the other ingredients to the cocktail shaker, I gave it a quick shake and poured the daiquiris into two martini glasses, filling them up to the brim. "Sounds like he might have been leading you on."

"Do you think so?"

Warning bells went off in my mind. My motto was don't get involved, especially in people's personal lives. It rarely went well. "On second thought, no. He's a friendly guy. I bet he doesn't realize the vibes he's giving off." I thought of the way he'd looked at me the last time I'd seen him. I might have misinterpreted his intentions too. "It's easy to get the wrong idea sometimes."

She smiled, seemingly reassured. "Thanks. I don't have lots of girlfriends to talk to."

I passed her one of the daiquiris carefully to avoid spilling it. She shifted Mr. Whiskers to her other arm and took the drink.

After a tentative sip, she grinned. "Mmm... That's even better than a strawberry daiquiri."

"Wait until you try one of my Mai Tais."

After the Mai Tais came Cosmopolitans. I only took a few sips of each drink, wanting to stay relatively sober until Bobbie came home. Jenna slurped them down like they were fruit punch. That's when I learned that Jenna couldn't handle her liquor. She snuggled her face in Mr. Whiskers' fur. "I like hanging out with you."

"Who? The cat?" I knew it was time to cut her off by the way her eyelids drooped.

"No," Jenna giggled. "You, silly. You're totally cool, not all stuck up like some people say."

Drunk people said all kinds of things, but I couldn't help asking, "Like who says?"

She waved a hand as if to dismiss my concern. "Do you think I'm too clingy? Luke says I'm too possessive. Like when he was hanging out with Sheila."

Now she had my attention. "He hung out with Sheila?"

"Yeah." She closed her eyes and I thought maybe she'd fallen asleep. Mr. Whiskers' eyes widened as her grasp on him loosened.

I gave her a little nudge and her eyes popped open.

She clutched Mr. Whiskers closer, then blinked a few times as if trying to remember what she'd been saying.

"What about Luke and Sheila?" I prompted.

Her brow furrowed. "I really didn't like Sheila. She strung him along for a while, saying she wanted to invest in his career. He's very talented you know."

"Yes, I know. What happened with Luke and Sheila?"

She sighed, her mouth in a tight line. "He figured out she wasn't really interested in helping him with his music business, so he started avoiding her. She found some other boy toy to torment, I guess."

I felt uncomfortable knowing that Luke and Sheila had been involved, although it helped explain the checks she'd written him. I'd have to ask him about her and the money. That would be an awkward conversation.

She sighed again. "She's dead, you know."

"Yeah, I know."

"I suppose I shouldn't talk bad about her. Do you think they'll find out who killed her?"

"If the police don't, Bobbie will." Oops. Maybe I should have kept that information to myself.

"I heard she wanted to be a detective. Like for real. What a funny rumor."

"Ha ha, isn't it?" I didn't mind Bobbie having a hobby, but I'd prefer one that didn't get her killed.

I parked Jenna on the sofa where she promptly fell asleep with Mr. Whiskers curled up in the crook of her arm, then I texted Bobbie to find out when she planned to come home. I heard a buzzing from the kitchen. Her phone sat on the charger where she'd plugged it in the night before.

"Dammit." She had an address book somewhere. Apparently when you became a senior citizen you were required to get one—maybe it came in the mail with your AARP card. I found hers in a drawer and searched for Rosa's number.

When Rosa answered, she informed me Bobbie had left an hour earlier. "I offered to give her a ride, but she wanted to walk. She's so independent."

I thanked Rosa and hung up, chuckling to myself since I knew the real reason Bobbie had turned down the offer of a ride. She'd told me Rosa's driving terrified her.

I stopped laughing. Rosa's house couldn't be more than a five-minute walk from home. Where was Bobbie?

I looked up Nancy's number in the address book and dialed, but it went to voice mail. Bobbie wouldn't be so foolish as to go see Nancy on her own, would she? I woke up Jenna to tell her where I was going. She nodded, said "sure," then fell back asleep. I left a note for Bobbie to call me if she came home before I returned.

My navigation sent me in the wrong direction down twisting mountain roads, many of them dead ends. As my frustration increased, I finally pulled up in front of a small cabin covered in redwood siding.

Parking the car several yards away, I approached the house as stealthily as possible. Bushes hid the windows on the left, so I kept to that side, slipping behind the foliage. The curtains on the first two windows were drawn tight. Moving toward the back of the house, the next window I came to looked in on an empty bedroom.

A rapping sound caught my attention, and I crept

toward the front of the house in time to hear Bobbie's voice. I kept out of sight and strained to listen.

"I'm looking for my granddaughter," Bobbie said. "Is she here?"

"Hello, Bobbie," Nancy replied. "Come on in. I was about to make a cup of tea. Oh, you brought your little dog. Such a cutie."

Darn. Had Bobbie gone home and seen my note? She must have taken a short cut available only by foot. Why couldn't she have just called me like I'd asked? With my car parked nearby, she would assume I was inside Nancy's house. Now what? Knock on the door?

At least Kit was there to protect her, but what could that little mutt do if things got ugly? If only I could be a fly on the wall, I might be able to learn something before Nancy realized we suspected her of murder.

I stepped back to look up at the second floor where a curtain fluttered in the breeze from an open window.

The pine trees stood several feet from the house, probably for fire safety, but one had a long limb that stretched out nearly touching the roof. I ran toward the tree and leapt for the lowest branch, grabbing hold for just a moment before I slipped back to the ground.

My palms were scraped from the bark, and I knew if I tried again, I'd be likely to draw blood. I pulled off my jacket and draped it over the branch, pulling myself up. The rest of the climb was easy. The limb I'd seen seemed strong enough to hold me, so I shimmied along it until I found myself dangling over the roof. I let go, landing on the shingles. Laying on my belly, I crept to the edge, looked over the side, and then slid sideways until I was right above the open window. I reached for the gutter and gave it a nudge, testing its strength.

Sucking in a deep breath, I went for it, swinging over the side of the roof. I clung to the gutter and rocked back and forth gaining momentum. One final thrust and I swung myself into the bedroom, doing a tuck and roll when I hit the ground.

I scampered to the door to see if I'd been heard. The longer it took before Nancy figured out I was inside her house the better.

Nancy's voice came from downstairs. "Did you hear something?"

"Must be some critter on the roof." Bobbie replied. "Or a tree limb scraping. I get that all the time at my house." No time to wonder if Bobbie realized I'd made the noise, I slipped out into the hall and tiptoed to a landing with stairs leading downstairs.

I heard Nancy say, "It's your own fault. If you'd just let me be a Ukulele Lady, I wouldn't have had to do what I did."

My grandmother's voice sounded surprisingly calm. "And what did you do, Nancy? I know you killed Martha. Did you kill Sheila too?"

Nancy's voice rose. "I didn't kill anyone." She sounded unhinged to me, and I wondered if she was telling the truth.

"Not on purpose, I'm sure," Bobbie replied.

I stepped closer to get a better look. Nancy stood in the middle of the living room holding a gun.

I took another step and cringed when the floorboard underneath me creaked loudly. I pulled back, but too late.

"What are you doing in my house uninvited, Whitley? Come on down and join us, won't you?"

Now I'd done it. I took the steps slowly, my mind working furiously trying to figure out how to get us out of this mess.

Kit ran straight for me, barking and wagging her tail. Nancy pointed her gun from Bobbie to me, and I worried that any sudden move might cause her to pull the trigger.

"Stop it, girl," I commanded, but Kit had a mind of her own. She ran toward Nancy, barking with excitement just as Bobbie tried to grab Nancy's gun. The gun went off, and I heard a scream. It might have been my own.

Kit lay on the floor in front of Nancy.

Chapter Eighteen

Nancy cried out, "Oh no! I shot the poor dog!" She wailed as if she'd been shot herself.

Bobbie yelled at her. "How could you? How could you shoot a poor defenseless dog?"

"Kit?" I took a few steps closer, bending down next to the little ball of fur. Hoping to catch Nancy off guard, I sprung up and punched her in the belly. She bent over in pain, and I kicked the gun out of her hand. Bobbie grabbed her from behind, her arms around her waist.

Kit lay as still as if she were asleep. I'd seen her chest move and hoped beyond hope that she was okay. "Kit?"

Kit jumped to her feet, tail wagging, and I burst into tears. I reached out my arms and she jumped right up into them. She licked my neck and ears and I let her. "Stupid dog." I buried my face in her fur.

While we waited for the police to arrive, I borrowed a scarf from Bobbie and tied Nancy's hands behind her back just to be safe. Bobbie badgered her with questions, but she insisted she had nothing to do with Martha's or Sheila's deaths, not even unintentionally.

"I put the snake in Vanessa's bathtub, and I put the baby oil on Rosa's back steps," she sobbed. "I just thought if they couldn't play in their groups, that there might be an opening for me. I didn't kill anyone."

"And Gypsy's fire?" Bobbie demanded. "She could have died from the smoke inhalation."

Nancy sniffled. "She wasn't supposed to be there that night. I never would have hurt Gypsy. I just thought if she had to rebuild her restaurant, she'd be too busy to play with the Ukulele Ladies."

Knowing her tears were because she'd been caught and not out of remorse, I had no sympathy for her. A little part of me blamed Bobbie and the others for excluding Nancy from participating in any of the groups, but that didn't justify her actions one bit.

When the police arrived, they had plenty of questions for us. I let Bobbie take the lead, filling in details when asked. As soon as they carted Nancy off to jail, I drove Bobbie back home. I couldn't decide whether to congratulate her or chew her out for going to a suspect's home by herself, so I said nothing.

As Bobbie led me through the twisted maze of streets, she asked, "Why is she willing to admit to what she did to Rosa, Vanessa, and Gypsy, but not Martha or Sheila?"

"Maybe because the jail terms for murder are a whole lot longer than they are for whatever she might be charged with for the other stuff. Arson and assault, perhaps? Malicious mischief?" I didn't know how long she'd spend in jail, but I hoped it would be a long time. "If they can't prove she killed anyone, then she might go to jail for a few years or maybe even get probation. I hope she gets help with her delusions, or whatever it is that drove her to do all that crazy stuff."

"I don't get it. Do you?" Bobbie asked as if I had all the answers. "I understand why she'd go after Martha. Maybe she didn't even intend for her to die. She was just so desperate to be a Ukulele Lady."

"She wanted to be in the Cougar Choir, too, remember? Sheila's death meant they had an opening as well."

She scoffed. "They never would have let her in, even if they did ask her to audition."

"Maybe, but she was delusional, so it's possible she thought of herself as a cougar." I thought of her in her jeans and tennis shoes and mentally pictured her with the sleek Cougars in their tight skirts and high heels. She would not have fit in.

"I suppose you're right," Bobbie said, but she didn't sound at all convinced to me.

I pulled into our driveway, surprised by how quickly we got home. As soon as I stepped through the door, I took a quick look around. "Where'd Jenna go?"

"I called her mother to come pick her up. How many drinks did you give her?" She gave me a scolding look.

"Just three. How was I to know she couldn't handle her liquor?" I refused to accept blame, although my drinks were almost too tasty to resist. "Speaking of drinks..." I could use a drink after all the excitement. "How about a daiquiri? No, never mind. We're out of limes. Hey, I have an idea. We should plant a lime tree."

"Sure, Whitley. I'll get right on that." Her voice oozed sarcasm.

I figured I'd ignore her attitude, considering she'd had a long day and it wasn't even four o'clock. I put the rum away and poured us each a glass of wine.

Holding the two glasses, I plopped on the sofa while she lit the fire. "I'm sorry about Nancy. It must be a big shock to find out your friend is a murderer."

As soon as the logs began to catch, Bobbie sat down and took the wineglass from me. She stared into the fledgling flames. "What if we're missing something?"

"Like what?" We'd caught a murderer, what more did she want?

"What if Nancy's telling the truth?" She turned to me, worry showing in her eyes. "What if she didn't kill Sheila and Martha?"

I didn't want to say it, but someone had to. "Then someone is walking around town thinking they've gotten away with it."

She nodded and went back to staring at the fire. "Who else might have wanted Martha and Sheila dead?"

"Someone else who wanted them out of the competition?" I suggested.

"That would be quite a coincidence if Nancy and another person both had the same motive, but one of them was willing to take more drastic steps." She tapped one finger on her lips, deep in thought.

"Well, you know Martha and Sheila better than I do. I never even met Sheila. What else did they have in common? Hobbies, friends, or... men?"

Bobbie raised her eyebrows. "Men?"

"Um, yeah. Were Martha or Sheila dating anyone? Besides whatever Sheila was doing with Luke, that is." I didn't really want to think about that. As for Martha, I couldn't picture her going on a date, but what did I know about what seniors did in their spare time?

"Sheila dated all the time." She lifted her glass to her lips, taking another sip. "She mostly liked her men young or rich, like most of the women in the cougar choir. I'm not judging, mind you. That's how I like my men too." Before I could object, she added, "And you do too, don't pretend otherwise."

"I like them my age, which happens to be relatively young at the moment." I hoped when I grew older, I wouldn't go chasing after young ones. "And there are worse things than being rich. What about Martha? Did she date?"

"She went out with Ralph once or twice, but I think it was purely platonic."

"Did Ralph ever date Sheila?" I asked.

"He did take her out a few times last year." Her eyes narrowed. "You can't think..." She left the thought unfinished, but I got her drift.

I shrugged, guessing she didn't want to consider Ralph as a suspect. "It's something the two victims had in common. And you said Ralph was handy. It would take someone handy to figure out how to electrify a puddle like they did in Martha's basement."

Bobbie gave an exaggerated shiver. "Don't call them victims, please. It gives me the willies."

"Okay. Martha and Sheila both dated Ralph. What else did they have in common?" Knowing what little I did

165

about sweet Martha and man-hunter Sheila, I couldn't imagine what hobbies or interests they might share.

"I can't think of anything right now." She frowned. "But I refuse to believe that Ralph is involved."

"Fine." That just meant I'd have to do my own background check on him. "I still think Nancy killed Martha and Sheila, but if she didn't... then we've still got a murderer to catch." And Ralph had a big crush on my grandmother. If he was a killer, she might not be safe.

"Oh, crap," I said, looking at the time. "I told Gypsy I'd bartend tonight. I'll call back and cancel."

"Why?" Bobbie asked. I gave her my best smirk, and she said, "You can't put your life on hold indefinitely. It could be a while until we figure this out."

After more discussion, Bobbie convinced me to go, agreeing to lock all the doors and not answer the door if someone came knocking.

"And I mean *anyone*," I added for emphasis.

I put on the Valentino shirt I'd snagged from my mother without her knowledge. Every girl needed a basic white shirt, and I'd been too proud to step into a Walmart, even though I had a budget so tight it squeaked. I reluctantly left the house after more reassurances from Bobbie.

A few minutes before five, I stepped through the front door of Gypsy's Tavern, and Elijah greeted me with a grateful smile. "Thanks so much for helping out."

"Happy to do it."

He showed me around the bar, explaining the setup. "It's mostly five-dollar draft beer and glasses of wine and whatever our cocktail special is until happy hour is over. Saturdays the special is Gypsy Punch. It's a rum punch in case anyone asks. I already made two pitchers. Just fill a highball glass with ice and pour to about an inch below the rim."

"Got it." This would be a lot easier than the Hotel Elegance where pretty much everyone wanted some sort of frou-frou drink or a martini made a certain way—and heaven forbid you got it wrong. As a bonus, I didn't have to dress like a slutty cavewoman like my last bartending gig.

"After happy hour, you'll mostly get beer and wine orders, along with the basic vodka tonics and scotch on the rocks. We don't get a lot of high rollers here." He pointed out the bargain liquor used for well drinks.

A couple entered the restaurant, and Elijah came out from behind the bar to greet them and show them to a booth. I checked out the selection of house wine and reviewed the liqueurs so I wouldn't waste time looking for them if someone ordered a fancy drink.

"Two draft Coors," he called out as he passed the bar. He ducked into the kitchen to put in their food order. When he returned, he picked up the two mugs I'd poured and delivered them to the table.

I'd settled in for a quiet evening when, just before six, the tables and bar filled with locals arriving at the tail end of happy hour for a cheap drink and appetizers. It was nonstop for over an hour, and then most of them cleared out, heading somewhere else for the evening. The next wave, mostly couples, lingered over dinner, and a few solo men ate at the bar. Most were regulars from what I could tell, greeting each other with fist bumps and making idle chit-chat.

"It'll be quiet now until the band shows up," Elijah said. "They start playing at nine."

"Luke's band?"

"It's not actually his band, but he plays in it," he said. "You know him pretty well?"

There seemed to be something implied between the lines. "I knew him when we were kids." I figured I might as well see if I could get some gossip out of Elijah. "He and Jenna seem pretty close."

He smirked. "That girl's been throwing herself at him ever since he came back to town. He acts like he's oblivious, but I don't know if I'm buying it, you know what I'm saying?"

I sure did. Maybe Luke liked having a groupie.

"Does Ralph ever come in here?" I asked.

"Ralph? From Peak Experience?" When I nodded, he said, "Sometimes he stops in after closing. Usually with a woman. For an old guy, he's kind of a player." He grinned, adding, "Nice guy," as if afraid I'd get the wrong idea.

"Who's he been in with lately?"

"Why so curious?" he asked.

"No reason," I lied. If I could talk to his latest squeeze, maybe I could find out a little more about how he treated his women. Mostly, I wanted to know about his temper and whether he was the jealous type. I couldn't think of any other motive he might have had to kill Sheila and Martha.

I felt guilty thinking bad things about Ralph at all. Elijah was right—he was a nice guy. But someone killed the two women, and my gut told me it was someone they both knew, probably well.

Luke arrived shortly after eight, along with the other band members. He seemed surprised to see me behind the bar, and after he put his saxophone case down, he came over to the bar to say hi.

He gave me a warm smile. "Are you working or just pretending to tend bar so you can get free drinks?"

I laughed. "You're onto me."

He motioned for me to come closer. I leaned in, and he whispered in my ear, "I won't tell anyone your secret." I felt his breath against my neck and goosebumps crawled down my arm. Since when had I been so affected by the proximity of a man? Six months of celibate life can do that to a girl.

Elijah spoke over my shoulder. "I'm surprised Jenna isn't here. She hardly ever misses a night when you're playing."

I tried not to snicker but couldn't help myself. "She's probably nursing a hangover."

"Is that so?" Luke asked.

"My fault," I admitted. "I forgot that some people don't know when to cut themselves off. Plus, I make some seriously yummy drinks."

Elijah gave me a smile. "I'll have to try you out one of these days."

That comment stopped me in my tracks, and I might have blushed. I swear he gave me a half wink before going to check on one of his tables.

Once the band started playing, conversation became limited to yelling. Elijah and I poured mugs of beer and mixed drinks, yelling, "What can I get you?" to patrons stacked three deep at the bar. I had plenty of bartending experience, but crowd control was new for me. After about an hour, the drink orders slowed, and things got back to a pace I could handle by myself.

When Luke and his group took a break, he came up to the bar. "How about a beer?"

I grabbed a mug. "How about you stop leading Jenna on?"

He seemed taken aback by my directness. "You think I'm leading her on?"

After pushing the beer toward him, I leaned my elbows on the bar. "Not everyone is immune to your charms, you know. A young, vulnerable woman is going to think that being nice means you like her. And by 'like her,' I mean interested."

He slid onto a barstool and took a sip of his beer. Something told me he knew how Jenna felt about him and hadn't needed me to tell him.

"She's a sweet girl," he said. "It's easy to be nice."

"Just be honest with her, and all the other young women who get crushes on you." I hoped he knew I didn't mean me, but before he could respond, I went to take an order at the other end of the bar.

One of the band members picked up his standing bass and began tuning it, so I figured I'd better ask Luke about Sheila while I had the chance.

"Another beer?" I asked, but he shook his head. I handed him a bottle of water. "You must have been upset when you heard about Sheila."

His eyebrows raised, but he answered dispassionately. "I think everyone in town was freaked out. They're saying she was murdered."

"Yeah, that's what I heard too. I also heard that you and she were close."

His jaw tensed. "What do you mean, close?"

"She invested in your career or something," I said, vaguely.

"Oh, that." His expression relaxed. "She loaned me the money to upgrade my home studio. Told me there was no rush to pay it back."

"Uh-huh." Now that she was dead, there was definitely no rush.

"Did Jenna say something to you?"

His question caught me off guard. I laughed it off. "People say a lot of things when they've had too much to drink."

"Jenna's nice and all that, but she has some... issues." He began to peel the edge of the label on his bottle of water.

"Like what?"

"She gets things in her head. It's almost like I can't even be friendly to her, or she thinks she's my girlfriend. She'll show up at my house and call me while she's standing in my front yard. Isn't that weird?"

"Yeah, weird." A thought occurred to me. "Does she get jealous?"

Luke shook his head slowly. "You have no idea. If I go on a date, I have to take them to Big Springs. Even then, one time she followed me there. I talked her into going to a therapist, and it's gotten somewhat better." he stood as the bass player strummed a few notes. "Sounds like my break is over."

The band resumed playing and normal conversation

came to an end. At least the crowd had died down, so my vocal cords might live to speak another day.

If Jenna thought Sheila was competition for Luke's affections, would that be enough to put her over the edge? I'd have to talk to Bobbie and see what else she knew about the young woman. I'd felt her obsessive affection firsthand.

Elijah joined me behind the bar. The door opened, and Ralph stepped inside, holding the door open for someone behind him. When Gypsy entered, I gave Elijah a questioning look, and he shrugged in response.

"They go out sometimes," he said as he pulled a pitcher of beer for one of the tables. "Dinner, drinks, stuff like that. Nothing serious."

Ralph and Gypsy perched on barstools, and I went to greet them. "Hi, you guys."

I made Ralph a vodka tonic and poured Gypsy a glass of wine. Doing my best to be subtle, I kept my eyes on them, watching for possessive or jealous signs from Ralph. They appeared relaxed and friendly, like two old friends keeping each other company. Maybe, at his age, Ralph just appreciated female companionship.

Elijah leaned over my shoulder. "I think I can handle it from here if you'd like to call it a night."

I gave him a grateful smile. My feet hurt, and I was beat. "Thanks. I think I'll take you up on that."

Chapter Nineteen

I woke up with the sun shining on my face. Had Bobbie let me sleep in for a change? Maybe she'd taken pity on me since I'd worked until after midnight. My phone buzzed and I read a text from my former coworker asking if I was still interested in renting a room from her. Her current roommate would be out by the end of November, only a week and a half away. We texted back and forth, and I got the particulars about rent and deposits.

I shuffled into the kitchen, grateful to find the coffee pot still warm. After filling my cup, I searched through the house for my grandmother and found her on the deck.

I caught her up on my evening working at Gypsy's. "Jenna seems really possessive about Luke," I said. "Do you think she might have done something crazy out of jealousy?"

She nearly choked on her coffee. "You think Jenna murdered Martha and Sheila? That little thing?"

"You don't?"

Bobbie didn't answer right away but her brow knitted as she thought it over. "Wait. Didn't she say that she and Mr. Chen were at the office all day when Martha was murdered? And they didn't even go to lunch?"

"Oh." There went that theory.

After filling her in on the rest of my evening, I segued into what I wanted to ask her. "I bet there's lots of bartending jobs in L.A., especially with the holidays."

She took a sip of her coffee. "Uh-huh."

"I have a friend with a room to rent." I kept going, planning to sell this idea. "It'll be available the first of December. I figured if I'm in L.A., it will be easier to network with people and I'll get back in with the studios a lot faster."

"What's the catch?" she asked, brows raised.

"Why do you always think there's a catch?" I heard the indignant tone in my voice.

"I don't always." She gave me an indulgent smile. "I know you, Whitley. Why do you forget that? I know when there's more to a story."

I sighed and leaned back in the chair. "Fine. I need to borrow some money. Unemployment ran out and I kinda went through most of my savings." There hadn't been much in my account before, but now it was cleaned out.

She opened her mouth to say something but shut it again. No doubt I had narrowly missed a lecture about saving money and living within my means. But it was hard to save money when you lived in Los Angeles. Everything was so darned expensive.

"How much?" she asked.

"About three thousand dollars." Four would be better, but I figured that might be pushing it.

She seemed to consider it, which I took as a good sign.

"There's something else." I paused, knowing she wouldn't like this part. "My mother doesn't want you to stay here alone. And she really wouldn't like it if she knew there's a murderer on the loose."

"Well, then. We just need to solve the murders before you move." Bobbie stood to go inside. When she reached the doorway, she turned back. "We can talk about this after Thursday."

At least she didn't say no. "What happens on Thursday?"

She frowned. "You really don't know that Thursday is Thanksgiving?"

"It is?" I had noticed Christmas decorations going up, but they did that earlier every year. "Does that mean you're cooking?"

"We're cooking."

Why my grandmother would want me in the kitchen was beyond me, considering my greatest cooking achievement was not burning frozen waffles. Then the realization hit me.

"No." I searched her face for a sign that my gut was wrong, but the smug look on her face told me otherwise. "*They're* coming?"

She nodded, and I closed my eyes, wanting to shut out the reality of the impending doom. My mind searched for a way to escape something I'd avoided for years.

Thanksgiving with my parents.

The heat from the stove enveloped me as I stirred the brown goo that would hopefully morph into delicious gravy, grateful to be in the kitchen and not the living room with my parents. I hoped Luke survived the encounter until I could rescue him. He'd planned to spend Thanksgiving alone until I impulsively invited him. Poor Luke. I should have warned him about my mother. I'd introduced him as a friend, but that wouldn't stop her from grilling him as if he were applying to be my future husband.

Rosa sat at the kitchen table folding napkins.

"How are you recuperating from your fall?" I asked, gesturing to the ACE bandage around her wrist.

"I'm doing much better," Rosa said. "The bandage is just to remind me not to overdo it. I'll be ready to play in the competition. It's just a few weeks away, you know."

Bobbie moved around me in a dance of pots and pans. The still-steaming turkey sat on the counter, filling the air with tantalizing aromas. Bobbie gently nudged me aside to put the dressing and green bean casserole in the oven.

"It's best not to cook the stuffing in the turkey," she informed me. "Less chance of food-borne illness if you cook it separately."

"Good to know." Another useless piece of information for my already overloaded brain. "But then it's not really stuffing, is it?" When I didn't get a reply, I asked, "How long do I have to stir this?"

She took the spoon from me and gave the thick liquid a quick stir. "Looks good. Hand me the gravy boat."

Rosa hopped up and grabbed it before I could,

handing it to Bobbie. "Everything smells wonderful." She reached for the turkey wing before Bobbie told her to sit back down.

My father walked into the kitchen just in time to carve the turkey, and I hurried to the living room to rescue Luke, surprised to find him laughing at whatever my mother had just said.

"There you are," she said. "I thought you were going to hide out all evening."

"I was helping Bobbie with dinner." Which is more than you offered, I wanted to add, but bit my tongue.

"Angela was telling me about the time you got invited to a princess party and you dressed up as Buffy the Vampire Slayer."

I glared at her. "She's way cooler than any Disney princess."

Luke gave me an appreciative smile. "I bet you rocked the crossbow."

"I totally did." I grabbed his arm. "Let me show you the deck."

My mother raised one imperious and perfectly shaped eyebrow. "Isn't dinner about to be served?"

"I need some fresh air. We'll be right back."

I grabbed Luke by the arm and led him onto the deck. The moment we stepped outside, I found myself overtaken by an urge to scream. Instead, I took a few deep breaths.

"You seem upset," he said.

I forced a smile. "Yeah. She just pushes my buttons."

"Really?" He looked back toward the living room. "She seems super nice."

I didn't want to talk about her. I just wanted the evening to be over with. We stood staring out at the forest in silence. The trees rustled softly in the chilly breeze, and my overheated body quickly cooled. I rubbed my arms. The temperature was barely above freezing, and I hadn't thought to grab a jacket before escaping.

Luke, always the gentleman, took off his jacket and wrapped it around my shoulders.

"Thanks," I said, gratefully. "Do all parents drive their kids crazy, or just mine?"

"Pretty sure it's a requirement." He took my hand and gave it a gentle squeeze. "When you love someone, it can make you a little crazy."

Something about the look in his eyes made me catch my breath. Before I could formulate a response, Bobbie opened the sliding glass door and summoned us to the dinner table. My mother took the chair next to Luke and motioned for me to sit across from her. My father took his spot at the head of the table, with Rosa between him and Bobbie. The table held a feast, even more impressive because Bobbie had prepared it by herself with only my help, which is to say, very little.

As I filled everyone's wine glasses, there were the usual compliments from my parents and Luke about how wonderful everything looked.

My father gave the obligatory toast, full of vague homilies about family and gratitude. I was grateful he skipped the part where we go around the table saying what we were thankful for. Soon we filled our plates and began eating in wonderful silence. I should have known it wouldn't last.

As I took my last bite, my father addressed Bobbie. "I've been meaning to ask you. Did you know the woman whose body was found nearby? Just last week, wasn't it?"

Angela dropped her fork and it clattered against her china plate. "Someone found a body? In Arrow Springs?"

"Whitley found it," Rosa said.

Chapter Twenty

I would have kicked Rosa if my legs were long enough but settled for a piercing glare. What was she thinking?

"Whitley found a dead body?" Angela's voice rose an octave. "And I'm just now hearing about it?"

"Kit found the body, actually," I said. "I just happened to be there. She'd been dead over a month if it makes you feel better."

"No, it does not make me feel better." She turned to Rosa. "Do dead bodies regularly turn up in this town?"

Rosa seemed to shrink in her chair. "Just lately, and there were only two." When my mother didn't yell, she appeared to gain confidence, and added, "Whitley found Martha's body, too, but that time Bobbie was with her."

Angela pushed her chair back and stood but didn't make a move to leave the table. Not moving her head, her eyes moved from Bobbie to me then back to Bobbie. "You're coming to stay with us." If her forehead could move after all the injections she'd had, her brows would be knitted in anger. The look in her eyes made up for it. "Both of you."

"I'm already planning to move back to L.A.," I said. As convenient as my parents' Beverly Hills home would be, not to mention the attraction of free rent, if I moved in with my mother, there would soon be another dead body. I didn't want to spend the rest of my life in jail for manslaughter.

"And I'm not going anywhere." Bobbie stood and began clearing plates.

I jumped at the chance to help and took the dishes from Bobbie.

Luke followed me into the kitchen. "You didn't tell me you were moving back to L.A. When is that happening?"

"Soon as possible." Did I imagine that he seemed disappointed? I gave him an apologetic smile. "I only just decided." And I still needed cash to make the move, or I wasn't going anywhere.

Bobbie carried more dishes in, piling them in the sink. She avoided making eye contact with me as if I'd done something wrong. Maybe she'd forgotten my poor track record with Angela. I'd never gotten my mother to change her mind about much of anything.

As I filled the coffee carafe with water, Angela entered the kitchen, looking out of place. In her world, kitchens were inhabited by servants. Bobbie ignored her scowling gaze, so Angela turned to me. "I'll be back for the two of you Sunday morning. Please be ready."

"This is my home," Bobbie said. "You can't force me to leave it."

My mother's lips tightened into a straight line as she fought to hide any sign of emotion. "As you know, your son and I are well placed in the community. We have connections. Lawyers and judges. If you continue to act irrationally—"

"Irrationally?" Bobbie's voice, louder than I remembered hearing it, boomed with indignation. She struggled to control herself, and when she spoke again, her voice was calm and steady. "I am of sound mind and body, and I can get twenty witnesses to testify to that."

"Including me," I said, hoping I wouldn't regret speaking up.

Angela's voice, cold as ice, gave me a shiver. "We'll see who the judge listens to—your so-called witnesses or my doctors and consultants."

Bobbie's eyes narrowed. "You wouldn't."

"I would."

I stood like a statue as my mother gave me a peck on the cheek.

"I'll be back Sunday. Be ready." She took a step in Bobbie's direction, but my grandmother jerked away from her.

Angela turned and walked into the living room and announced to my father that they were leaving.

My father, in a surprised voice, replied, "We are?"

I watched from the kitchen doorway as my parents put on their coats. My father, looking confused, kissed me on the cheek, and told me to take care of myself.

Once they left, Rosa insisted on helping Bobbie do the dishes, and I joined Luke on the sofa in front of the fire. I stared at the flames as they crackled, not sure why

I let my mother get to me. After all these years, I thought I'd become immune. Maybe I was out of practice.

"You okay?" Luke asked.

"Sure, why wouldn't I be?" I'd planned to leave Arrow Springs as soon as possible anyway. "It's Bobbie I'm worried about."

He patted my hand, then stroked it gently from my wrist to my fingers. "I hoped you'd stick around a bit longer. I was getting used to having you around."

I felt a tingle up and down my arm but told myself not to get carried away.

"I'm sure you and Bobbie have a lot to talk about. I'll give Rosa a ride home." He rose from the sofa. "Call me if there's anything I can do."

He held my gaze, a slight smile on his lips. What nice lips he had. I could think of one or two things he might be able to help with, but that would have to wait until later. Right now, Bobbie needed me.

After Luke and Rosa had left, I returned to the kitchen where Bobbie held a large, sharp-looking knife.

"Violence is not the answer," I said. "As appealing as it may seem."

Bobbie made some sort of sound between a huff and a groan, perhaps meant to exorcise the stress and anger built up from her confrontation with Angela.

She pointed the knife toward the counter. "I'm cutting the pumpkin pie. Do you want a piece?"

"Might as well make it a double, since we don't have to share."

She cut the pie into oversized slices while I retrieved

the whipped cream from the refrigerator. I covered my pie in as much topping as the plate would hold.

Bobbie did the same, then pointed the nozzle at her mouth and injected herself with a large dose. "I've always wanted to do that."

We took our pie and coffee back to the dining room table where a few remnants of our feast remained. I grabbed a fork and dug in.

"Mmm..." While I shoveled pie into my mouth, Bobbie stared at her slice as if she'd forgotten what it was for.

I couldn't take seeing my grandmother looking so forlorn. "What's wrong?"

Her eyes darted to mine. They were full of anger and sadness and something else I recognized. Abandonment. Bobbie, the one person in my life who had never abandoned me, who had stood up for me even to her own detriment, was being abandoned.

By me.

A wave of feelings crashed over me, a completely unpleasant feeling after so many years of stuffing feelings down somewhere where they wouldn't bother me. Apparently, no matter how hard you stuff emotions, they don't go away. They just fester until one day they reappear out of nowhere. I didn't need complicated feelings to get in the way right now, but there they were.

I took a deep breath, hoping it would steady my voice. "I won't leave you."

She glanced up at me and blinked, then stared back at her pie before answering. "I know being stuck in the mountains with an old lady isn't how you envisioned your life."

"That's true." My life for the last few weeks hadn't been anything I would have ever imagined for myself. Fresh air, small-town gossip, and chasing after a murderer were all new for me. "I've actually been having fun. I mean, not the finding bodies part, but the rest of it—going around questioning people, chasing down clues... I thought my old life was exciting, but most of what I do is wait around for someone to tell me to take a punch or fall out a window. I love the adrenaline rush, but that's over in a minute."

"The way you describe it, it sounds a lot like sex."

I laughed. She had a point. "Yeah, but I keep going back for more."

She stabbed her pie with a fork. "When I start my detective agency, maybe you'll come back and help from time to time."

I didn't want to say too much, but I couldn't help myself. "Or maybe I'll stay here and go back to L.A. for stunt jobs from time to time. I haven't made any decisions yet—"

Bobbie jumped up, nearly knocking over her chair, and threw her arms around my shoulders in an awkward, sideways hug.

"Whoa," I said as she nearly crushed my larynx. "I'm not ready to commit."

She laughed. "The day you're ready to commit to anything is the day I check to make sure a Whitley robot hasn't taken your place. All I want from you is today. Well, and the rest of the weekend, up until your mother drives up here thinking she's going to take us back with her."

"What's the plan?" I asked. "You know she doesn't take no for an answer."

She crossed her arms over her chest, a determined expression on her face. "We need to solve Sheila's and Martha's murders. ASAP. Not only do I not want to move in with my son and Angela, but the contest is in two weeks."

By the time I'd demolished a second piece of pie, Bobbie had torn several pages out of a spiral notebook and spread them out on the table.

At the top of one, in big letters, she'd written John Chen. I pointed out that we hadn't uncovered any connection between the real estate agent and Sheila. Also, he had an alibi.

"Jenna might have lied for him," she said. "I don't believe he's our killer, but in the interest of thoroughness, I'm including him."

I nodded. "It's good to be thorough."

She glanced at me suspiciously, no doubt wondering if that was one of my famously sarcastic remarks. She wasn't used to supportive, affirming Whitley.

Next, she wrote Nancy's name on top of another sheet of paper. "She admits to sabotaging Rosa's steps, intending for her to fall and be injured and starting Gypsy's fire, but she's not fessing up to either murder." She wrote a few illegible scribbles on the sheet.

"I tend to believe her," I said. "Not because of her honesty, mind you, but I don't think she would have been strong enough to kill Sheila, drag her to the forest, and bury her."

"Very true, dear. I've often had to help her move the furniture so she could vacuum behind the chairs. In the future, I think..." Her voice drifted off, and a wistful expression came over her. "I just realized I'll need to find a new cleaner. Oh, well. Life must go on."

"What do you think about Jenna?" I asked. "If Mr. Chen's alibi is in question, then so is Jenna's. Luke says his relationship with Sheila was strictly platonic, but if Jenna thought they were involved—"

"You don't think they were?"

I stiffened, realizing I felt defensive at her implication. I couldn't imagine Luke being a killer, but if we were going to get anywhere, I'd need to keep an open mind. "Luke says they had a business relationship. She had invested in his career."

Bobbie nodded thoughtfully. Was she keeping something from me?

"Do you know something I don't?" I asked.

"No, no, nothing like that." Her scribbles had deteriorated into doodles. "You like him, don't you?"

"Sure. He's nice enough." I didn't want to give my feelings away, especially since it seemed unlikely anything would come of them. "Don't you like him?"

"That's not what I mean, and you know it." She tried to look serious, but a half smile played on her lips.

"Number one," I began, "I'm not ready for a relationship, especially with things up in the air the way they are. Number two, I'm not talking about my love life with my grandmother."

"Afraid you'll learn something?" She snickered.

"What? No." I got up and refilled my wineglass, returning to the table with the bottle. "Let's get back to business." I took the paper with Jenna written on top and made my own notes. Potential stalker. No boundaries.

Overly perky.

Bobbie watched me write. "Since when did perky become a red flag."

"It's the 'overly' part that is the problem. It's not normal."

Bobbie took the page from me. "Is she strong enough?"

"Yep. I've seen her bench press eighty pounds. I think she could drag a body or dig a shallow grave."

"But why would she kill Martha?"

"Do I have to figure out everything? Maybe Martha knew something, and Jenna had to get rid of her."

Bobbie didn't seem impressed with my theory.

I leaned back in my chair. "Okay, if it's not Jenna, then who?"

Bobbie took a blank sheet of paper and wrote at the top of the page in big letters. When she turned it around, I saw that she'd written "Luke."

Two could play that game. I took another sheet of paper and wrote in large letters, "Ralph." I passed it to her.

"Ralph? You're still on that kick?"

"He dated Martha and Sheila." A memory suddenly stabbed me in the gut—the last time I saw Ralph. I gasped.

"What's wrong?"

I grabbed her arm. "I hope Gypsy's not in danger. I saw them together at her bar last weekend. It seemed totally casual, but he might be putting on an act, waiting to get her alone, and then whammy!" I smacked the table for emphasis.

Bobbie jumped, spilling her coffee. "Don't ever do that again."

⋯⋯

Some people get up early on Black Friday and hit the stores. I put on an extra big pot of coffee while Bobbie invited two of the Ukulele Ladies over.

Rosa showed up with breakfast burritos and Gypsy brought cinnamon rolls. I was starting to enjoy hanging out with my grandmother's friends. Kit must have smelled the food, because she stayed close by, hoping for a handout.

Bobbie slipped bacon to the dog under the table while she brought the women up to speed and presented them with our suspects.

"Ralph?" Gypsy seemed taken aback. "That's ridiculous. What a sweet man. Why is he a suspect?"

Bobbie pointed a thumb at me. "Whitley thinks he should be on the list because he dated Martha and Sheila."

"He's dated every woman in town. Except you, Bobbie." Gypsy said. "If he went wacko and decided to kill someone, it would probably have been you just because you kept turning him down. Talk about unrequited love."

"Look," I said. "We all need to keep an open mind."

Bobbie nodded. "I know. But I'm just not willing to believe that Ralph is a murderer."

Rosa picked up the paper with Ralph's name. "Me neither."

"I think Mr. Chen did it," Bobbie said, "but Whit says he has an alibi. So much for an open mind."

"Hey," I objected. "I'm not the one who said he was in his office the entire day of the Fossil Fest. Jenna did."

"That's right," Bobbie said. "But how do we know she's telling the truth?"

"Why would Jenna lie and give Mr. Chen an alibi?" Gypsy asked. "Do you think he asked her to cover for him?"

"She might have been covering for herself," Bobbie said. "Did you ever think of that?"

I considered the idea. "That would have been thinking two steps ahead, and I don't think she's that clever. I mean she's not stupid, but, well..."

"She's no rocket surgeon," Gypsy agreed. "That's for sure."

"Scientist," Bobbie corrected. "Rocket scientist."

"Isn't that what I said?"

I lined up the pages with the suspects' names. Only one person remained no one had mentioned, almost as if we were all avoiding it. Luke.

"I saw Luke at the Fossil Fest right before we opened the booth at five." We'd reminisced about our younger years, and he'd flirted with me. I was pretty sure I'd flirted back. "Who would kill someone, then go to a festival and chat up an old friend, knowing the body might be discovered any moment?" I shuddered.

I shuffled through the sheets of paper again, as if I could deal a better hand. "There must be someone else. Someone we haven't thought of yet."

Bobbie sent me to the General Store for a whiteboard

and erasable markers. As long as I was there, I ordered some sandwiches from the deli counter. It might take us all day to solve the murder, and I wanted to make sure our brain cells had plenty of fuel. Peanuts were full of protein and those "good" fats I kept hearing about, and chocolate had antioxidants, so I grabbed a family-size bag of peanut M&Ms.

When I returned, I found Gypsy and Rosa huddled at the table making notes. "Have you made any progress?" I asked.

Bobbie grabbed the shopping bag from me and took it into the kitchen. "Thanks for thinking of food. I'm so distracted, I didn't even realize it was nearly lunchtime."

"That's understandable." I followed her into the kitchen. "It feels like we just had breakfast."

"We're trying to come up with another suspect," she explained as she pulled the sandwiches out of the bag. "Or, I should say, I am. Those two make terrible sleuths."

"What have you come up with?" I reached for a sandwich, but she smacked my hand.

"It could be a stranger," she said casually. "Grab some glasses." She pulled a pitcher of iced tea from the refrigerator.

"You mean like a random serial killer?" I didn't want to think about a serial killer roaming the streets of Arrow Springs. "That doesn't make sense. Don't serial killers usually use the same methods for all their victims?"

"I suppose so," she said, sounding disappointed that her theory didn't hold water.

While she cut up the sandwiches into smaller pieces

to share, I talked her through potential clues. "When we went to Martha's, the door was locked, right?"

"Yes, but that doesn't mean anything since you pointed out to me that the killer could have used the spare key. If that's how they got in, then they locked it when they left and put the key back to cover their tracks."

"But who would have known where she kept the key?"

She shrugged. "Even if someone didn't know, it wouldn't have been too hard to find."

"Okay." We weren't getting anywhere just talking. "We need to find out which of our suspects have alibis and whether they check out. We need to find out if Ralph was at his restaurant earlier that day."

"I can go ask him," Bobbie said.

"Not alone." My nerves were frayed as it was. I couldn't take much more of this kind of excitement. "Take Rosa and Gypsy with you."

"And a gun," she added.

"No! No guns."

She gave me a sly smile. "Just kidding."

We carried the sandwiches into the other room and set the tray on the table. Rosa looked up from her phone with a guilty face.

"What are you two doing?" Bobbie asked, a scolding tone to her voice.

"Just sharing pictures of our grandkids," Gypsy said, not sounding the least bit contrite. "We haven't gotten anywhere and needed something pleasant to think about."

Made sense to me. "Have a sandwich. Food always cheers me up."

Bobbie remained focused on the task at hand. "If we're going to find out who murdered Martha and Sheila—"

"Why aren't we letting the police handle this again?" Gypsy asked.

I thought it was a perfectly good question, but Bobbie huffed at her two friends. "If we don't solve these murders before Sunday, I'm going to be exiled to Beverly Hills."

"That sounds horrible," Gypsy said, not trying to hide her sarcasm.

"Out!" Bobbie waved at the two women. "I don't need you here if you're just going to distract us from the investigation."

"Fine," Gypsy said, giving Bobbie the side-eye. "I've got to go to work anyway." She motioned to Rosa. "Are you coming?"

Rosa gave Bobbie and me an apologetic look and followed Gypsy to the door.

I plopped down at the table and grabbed a sandwich, taking a big bite. "What are we supposed to do with all these sandwiches?"

Bobbie pulled out a chair and collapsed into it. "What are we supposed to do with all these clues? I feel like we're no closer than before."

A tap-tap came from the front door and Bobbie gave me a questioning look before going to answer it. She returned with Rosa.

"I want to help," Rosa said. "I don't want you to go away."

Bobbie seemed touched, but unwilling to show it, she gave Rosa a sly smile. "Is that just because the Ukulele Ladies have a chance to win for once?"

Rosa laughed. "Miracles can happen, you know." Her expression turned serious. "But tell me how I can help. I don't want you to have to leave town."

"Why don't we go talk to Jenna's mother together?" Bobbie turned to me. "That is if it's okay with my overseer."

I sighed. "Just stay safe, okay?"

"Of course," Bobbie said. "Let me grab my coat."

After spending the day talking about murder suspects and clues, I couldn't sit still. I kept thinking about the coincidence that Ralph had dated Martha and Sheila. My grandmother said she and Ralph were just friends, but it didn't take a genius to tell he was interested in more. If he'd killed the other two women, that meant my grandmother was in danger too.

Being in the house alone, I noticed every sound from the scraping of a tree on the roof to a creak from the deck. My phone buzzed with a text from Luke, and I asked him if he'd like to stop by. I could take care of myself, but maybe having someone in the house with me would make me less jumpy.

Sure, he was a murder suspect, but so were half the people in town at this point. Besides, I had good instincts about people. He might have made some questionable decisions when it came to Sheila, but I didn't believe for a moment he could have killed her. As for Martha, she was like a second mother to him. I made a pot of decaf while I waited.

"Coffee?" I asked when he arrived. He took a seat at

the kitchen table while I poured two cups, handing him one.

I got the milk from the refrigerator and joined him at the table. "I think Ralph might be the murderer." I wasn't much for small talk.

Luke stopped in the middle of pouring milk into his coffee. "Ralph? Are we talking about the same guy? Ralph?" he repeated, incredulous. "The guy who owns the Peak Experience?"

"Yes," I snapped, my frustration growing. I told myself that biting his head off wouldn't help anything.

"Hey, I'm on your side, remember?"

"Sorry. I'm a bit on edge." I took a deep calming breath. It didn't work. "He went out with both Martha and Sheila. Do you know where he lives?"

"Ralph isn't some psycho murderer," Luke protested. "He's a really nice guy."

"News flash. People don't go around advertising that they're a killer or wear special badges. Psychos are surprisingly good at appearing to be nice, regular guys." My patience was growing thin, like a rubber band just before it snaps. "Where does he live? Do you know or not?"

"I have no idea, but I could ask around. Have you tried to find his address online?"

I put my head down on the table, frustration getting the best of me. "His address isn't listed anywhere," I murmured before lifting my head. "I already checked."

Luke reached over and patted my hand. It felt surprisingly comforting. It was the sort of thing my grandmother would do. My mother didn't pat my hand or stroke my arm and say "there, there." For that, I had Bobbie. When

195

there's only one person who has ever loved you like that, how can you even think about letting them down?

For a moment, I'd stopped worrying about the killer. I needed to solve this murder whatever it took so Bobbie could stay in her home surrounded by friends.

I took a gulp of coffee and blinked hard, willing the tears not to fall. "Wait a second," I said. "We can follow him home. I bet he's still at the restaurant."

"Of course." Luke stood and grabbed his jacket. "Why didn't I think of that? Let's go."

He headed for the door. I pulled on my boots and hurried after him.

We stepped outside into the darkness. Luke headed to his car, but I stopped and stared down the dark street. No streetlights. No traffic.

"This isn't going to work," I said. "He'll spot our head-lights if we follow him."

"I hadn't thought of that. So, what do we do?"

"I wish we had a tracking device." I wondered if Bobbie had one in her private detective bag of tricks. I looked at my watch. It was almost nine o'clock, and I had no idea how late he would be at his restaurant. For all I knew, he'd already gone home.

Then it came to me.

"I can use my smartwatch!" I waited for Luke to tell me it was a stupid idea.

"Brilliant!" he said. "You're brilliant!" He grabbed me and planted a kiss right on my lips.

For a moment neither of us said a word, just stared at each other.

"Sorry," he said, finally. "I got excited. Let's go."

"We'll take my car." I wanted to be in control, or at least feel in control.

I drove to Ralph's restaurant, where we found his truck parked in the back. Luke kept an eye out while I strapped my watch to the bumper.

"Okay," Luke said. "Now what?"

"We wait. Should we go back to the house?"

"Let's stay nearby," he suggested. "Gypsy's is still open. Buy you a drink?"

A drink sounded great right now. "Sure. But just one. I need to stay sharp."

Gypsy greeted us from a barstool where she chatted with patrons. Elijah, standing behind the bar, glanced up as we entered, then went back to mixing cocktails.

"Grab a seat," Luke said. "What can I get you?"

I looked over at the bar and Elijah caught my eye. "I'll take an old fashioned." I grabbed a seat in the last booth. My booth.

I took out my phone and opened the "find my phone" app. It showed my watch still in the restaurant parking lot.

Luke sat down and set an old fashioned in front of me. I took a big sip and felt the warmth flow down my throat.

"You'll catch whoever killed Martha," Luke said. "I believe in you."

"Why do you care so much? I know Martha was your music teacher at school, but there must be more to the story."

"My parents got a divorce when I was fourteen," he said. "My mom wanted me to move to Ohio with her. Don't get me wrong, I love my mom, but music was everything to me. When my parents would fight, I'd put my headphones on and listen to Miles Davis or Bach, or Green Day, just to block out the sound. Music saved me."

I didn't know what to say to that. I knew all about being saved. When my gymnastics career imploded, I don't know what I would have done if I hadn't found parkour and free running. When I became a stunt double, I began to feel alive again, like I'd found a place where I fit in the world.

"You must have had lots of music teachers," I said. "What made her special?"

He stared at his drink as he spoke. "She found out I had a record player, and she loaned me all of her old LPs. Records," he added, possibly not sure I'd know what an LP was. "She introduced me to all the great jazz musicians and opened my eyes, or maybe I should say ears, to a whole world of music I never would have known about. I'd stay after class, and we'd just talk."

"And then you got back in touch when you came back to town?"

"We never got out of touch," he said with a smile. "We emailed all the time. She believed in me the way my parents never did." Tears welled up in his eyes, and he cleared his throat to hide his emotions.

"I'm sorry." I reached out and touched his hand briefly in what I hoped was a comforting gesture.

"Anyone believe in you like that?" he asked.

"My parents, briefly when I was on my way to becoming a star athlete. After I quit gymnastics, it took a long time before I started believing in myself again. It only happened when I started following my own dreams instead of everyone else's." I had learned to stand on my own two feet and not rely on anyone. I made sure no one relied on me too. At least I thought I had.

Gypsy rose from her stool and blew her son a kiss. "I'm off. Don't wait up." She winked at her son and gathered her belongings.

"Where is she going?" I asked Luke under my breath. "Do you think she has a date with Ralph?"

"How should I know?" He must have seen my concern because he spoke more loudly. "I left my wallet in the car. I'll be right back."

Minutes later, he returned to the booth. "She walked across the street to Ralph's restaurant."

"She might be in danger," I whispered. I glanced at the bar where Elijah looked away, pretending he hadn't been watching us.

I didn't care right now what he thought about Luke and me. Bobbie needed me to help her solve two murders, and I needed to make sure Gypsy was okay. I stared at the phone and saw the little dot representing my watch move on the screen.

"Let's go," I said. "He's on the move."

Chapter Twenty-One

We got in my car, and I handed Luke my phone so he could track where my watch and Ralph went. I kept his truck in sight until he turned down a dark street, and then I backed off, making sure he didn't see my headlights.

Luke directed me up and down dark, windy streets.

"Who designed the street system here?" I asked. "A six-year-old with a sense of humor? I feel like we're going in circles."

"I'm not sure 'designed' is the right word," he explained. "Not much planning involved. And we have been going in circles. Pull over for a minute."

Luke got out of the car and stared up at the hillside. I turned the car off and came around to stand next to him. Luke showed me the phone.

"It's close," I said. "But where?"

"Up there, somewhere, I think."

"There!" I pointed at a faint light from a house barely

visible through the trees. "There must be a road or driveway somewhere. We didn't see his truck on the street."

I grabbed a flashlight out of the glove compartment, and we walked along the street, looking for a way up to the house. My frustration was growing along with my anxiety. We had no idea what Ralph had planned for Gypsy.

"Should we call the cops?" Luke asked.

"And tell them what? That we think Ralph is a serial killer and we followed him to his house? We have no evidence that he's the murderer."

"Oh, I hadn't thought of that."

"I'm going to take the direct route," I said, and started up the side of the hill, wishing I'd worn hiking shoes instead of boots.

"Right behind you," Luke said.

We climbed through the trees and over rocks. In the light of the dim flashlight, I missed a rock and tripped, doing that thing where you wave your arms to keep yourself from losing balance. Luke grabbed me from behind as if I didn't feel awkward enough.

"You okay?" Luke asked.

"I was hoping you didn't see that."

We huffed and puffed our way up the hill until we reached a clearing where an impressive, two-story home stood. Ralph's truck sat in the driveway.

"Wow," I said. "Nice place."

I turned off the flashlight, and we made our way to the side of the house, guided by a three-quarter moon and a dim glow from inside the house.

Luke and I went from window to window in opposite

directions, trying to look inside, but all the curtains were drawn. I waited for him near the back door.

"Psst."

I turned to see Luke waving at me from around the side of the house.

"Can you see inside?" I whispered.

He nodded, and I crept to where he was. The windows were higher on this side—too high to see into. He'd found a bucket which he turned upside down.

He held my arm and helped me climb up so I could peer in through the window. "Gypsy's with him!"

It's possible I was louder than I should have been because Ralph turned toward the window. In my panic, not wanting to be seen, I tried to jump down, but it was dark, and I missed my footing.

It's also possible that I yelled a swear word or two when I fell. Luke must have tripped because I landed on top of him.

"Hold it right there," a man's voice commanded, and it didn't sound friendly. He shined a flashlight in our eyes, and I couldn't see his face in the glare, but I recognized Ralph's voice as I stared down the barrel of a rifle.

"Whitley?" He sounded confused. "Luke? What are you two doing trying to break into my house?"

I gave a weak laugh and climbed off Luke so he could stand.

"We were just passing by," I said holding my hands in front of my face to block the flashlight's glare. "Definitely not breaking into houses."

"Yeah," Luke added nervously. "Definitely not."

"Can you not shine the light right in our eyes?" I asked, realizing I wasn't in much of a position to make requests.

"Oh, sure," Ralph said, lowering the flashlight and the rifle.

I blinked to get rid of the spots, then I realized the spots were on Ralph's pajamas. I tried to connect the dots, so to speak.

"Is Gypsy here?" I asked.

"Gypsy?" He looked uncomfortable. "No, of course not. Why would she be here?"

"It's okay, Ralph," Gypsy said, coming up from behind him in a slinky robe.

I looked at Luke and gave him a "well, this is awkward" look, but he didn't seem to get my meaning.

"Why don't you two come inside," she said to us. "I'd better tell you about Ralph's alibi."

Ralph looked from Gypsy to me and back to Gypsy. "What's going on?"

"Nothing much," Gypsy said. "They just thought you might be a murderer."

Luke held my arm as we made our way down the hillside. We drove home in silence.

"What now?" he asked as I pulled up in front of Bobbie's house.

"I'm glad Gypsy's okay, but now we're back to square one. I was so sure it was Ralph. I'll have to see if Bobbie's still up and find out if she learned anything."

"What is she looking into?" he asked with a curious note in his voice.

"She's checking to see if we can find out if Jenna has an alibi."

"Jenna?" He sounded incredulous. "Next thing I know, you'll think I'm the killer."

I shrugged. "I never thought that for a moment."

His brows drew together as we locked eyes. "But Bobbie did?" When I didn't answer, he took a step back. He shook his head and walked toward his car.

I called after him. "But I stuck up for you."

As he drove away, Rosa's car pulled up and Bobbie got out. Bobbie waved goodbye and walked toward me.

"Was that Luke?" Bobbie asked. "I thought we weren't going to be alone with murder suspects."

"Do you really think Luke...?"

"Do you really think Ralph...?"

"No." I unlocked the front door. "Not anymore. Come on in and I'll tell you about my evening."

I told Bobbie about my adventurous evening and how I'd basically accused two people of murder. "I have a feeling my popularity in this town will plummet when word gets out."

"You think that's bad. Try accusing someone's daughter."

I gave her a sympathetic look. "Sounds like it didn't go well."

"That's an understatement. I don't think I'll be welcome at book club meetings in the future. Jenna told her mother she worked the day Martha died."

"We already know that's what she claims. We need to ask her boss if she was there the entire time."

"Tomorrow," Bobbie said. "There's nothing more we can do tonight."

In my dream, a drum pounded as I made my way through jungle vines, slashing at vegetation with a machete. The vines retaliated by smacking me in the face. I blinked awake, becoming aware that the smacking came from Mr. Whiskers swatting at my nose. The pounding came from our front door.

"Stop that," I scolded the cat. Kit must have heard me since she crawled out from under the covers. With a snarl from her and a hiss from Mr. Whiskers, they chased each other out of my room. I rolled out of bed wondering how late it was.

The pounding had stopped, and for a moment I thought I'd imagined it until it began again. I slid my feet into my slippers and made my way to the living room.

Through the peephole I saw Jenna, her hair sticking out in several directions, giving her a decidedly crazy appearance. Maybe if I ignored her, she'd go away.

"I know you're in there, Whitley!" she called out.

Was she just saying that, or did she recognize my car in the driveway? The chain on the door seemed secure, so I unlocked the door and opened it as much as the chain allowed.

"What are you doing here, Jenna?"

She put her face up to the narrow opening. "You think I'm a murderer."

"No, I don't," I said in the calmest voice I could muster. "You're one of many suspects. I can't let my personal feelings affect who we investigate and who we don't. Bobbie wants to be a private detective. What kind of detective would say, 'I'm not even going to consider her a suspect—she's such a nice young lady'?"

"Oh," she said, backing up enough so I felt somewhat less threatened. "I hadn't thought of it that way. Are a lot of people suspects?"

"Lots." When she didn't respond, I added, "Dozens."

My grandmother's voice called out behind me. "Who are you talking to?"

I turned to see her in a terry robe and towel turban. "It's Jenna."

She scowled at me as if I were being inhospitable by not immediately inviting a murder suspect into our home. "Well, let her in."

I hoped that between my grandmother and me we could handle Jenna if she suddenly turned homicidal. "Would it be rude to frisk her?" I whispered before I slid the chain and opened the door.

"Jenna, how nice to see you," Bobbie said in greeting. "What brings you by?"

"She doesn't like being a murder suspect," I said, speaking for Jenna.

"No one does," Bobbie said. "Come in and have coffee with us. I put on a pot to brew before I got into the shower."

Bobbie led us into the kitchen where Jenna took a seat, folding her hands in front of her on the table. I couldn't quite figure her out. She appeared the picture of innocence, a non-threatening entity. But I knew better. How far had her obsessiveness driven her?

"Nuts?" Bobbie asked.

I jerked around, only to see her holding a bowl of raw almonds, cashews, and hazelnuts.

"They're full of antioxidants and omega-3s," Bobbie continued. "Protein too. I think it's good to start the day with some protein."

"Thanks," Jenna said cheerfully, scooping up a handful.

Once everyone had their coffee and doctored it with cream and sugar, Bobbie joined Jenna at the table. I reluctantly took a seat, fighting my urge to flee.

"The coffee is delicious, Mrs. Leland," Jenna said.

"Please call me Bobbie." She launched into a dissertation on the benefits of organic and free-trade beans freshly ground to preserve the flavor. Jenna paid rapt attention while I let my mind wander, focusing on the young woman's body language. She appeared calm, with a relaxed posture, but she gripped her cup so tightly her knuckles whitened.

"—and that's why we considered you a prime suspect."

I came out of my reverie, wondering how much of the conversation I missed.

Bobbie continued in a soothing voice. "I hope you understand. It wasn't personal in the least. You seem like a sweet girl."

I wanted to say "ha!" but I kept my expression impassive to the best of my ability. Jenna's mouth turned up slightly in a tense smile, and her grip on the coffee cup relaxed slightly. My grandmother seemed to be attempting to calm our suspect enough that she might reveal more than she intended. I observed her technique to see how well it worked.

"Did you know Martha well?" Bobbie asked. "I'm hoping to get an outsider's view of the situation. I gather she and Luke were close."

"They were," she said. "He helped her with a lot of things around the house. He did that for a lot of the seniors in town who needed help. Like moving a sofa, things like that. He's very strong, you know."

I nodded but stayed quiet, not wanting to screw up Bobbie's line of questioning.

"Did you ever go to Martha's with him?" Bobbie asked. I had a feeling she knew the answer.

"I did once. That's how I knew Mr. Whiskers. Luke told me not to come with him again. He said she didn't like me." Her eyes began to water. "Why wouldn't she like me?" Her eyes moved from Bobbie to me, pleading for an answer.

Without thinking, I asked, "How did that make you feel?"

Her face fell. "How would you feel?"

I shrugged. "Lots of people don't like me. What do I care? I probably don't like them either."

She gave me an incredulous stare as if I'd said drinking water could kill you. It could, but only in huge doses.

"I'm a nice person," she said. "Why wouldn't someone like me?"

Because you're a psycho stalker maybe? "Did she or Luke give you a reason?"

She stared at her coffee cup as if she meant to do it harm before picking it up with both hands and taking a gulp. "Luke told me she thought I was perfid—perfid—"

"Perfidious?" Bobbie guessed.

I'd never heard the word. I leaned closer to Bobbie, asking her, "What does that mean?"

Jenna answered. "It means you can't be trusted. I had to look it up. I think she used a big word on purpose. Just because I don't know big words doesn't mean I'm stupid."

"Of course it doesn't," Bobbie agreed.

Jenna took another sip of coffee before quietly adding, "She laughed at me."

That didn't sound like the Martha I knew from our brief acquaintance. Still, people weren't always what they appeared to be.

"I'm sure she didn't mean to laugh at you, Jenna," Bobbie said. "Maybe you misunderstood her."

Jenna scowled. "I did *not* misunderstand her. I'm very good at understanding, I'll have you know."

It was nearly lunchtime when Bobbie gave Jenna a bag of nuts to take with her and walked her to the front door.

"Just one question, if you don't mind," I said before she stepped outside. "Is the real estate office open today?"

"No," Jenna said quickly. "Mr. Chen never works on the weekends."

"Do you know how we could get in touch with him?" I asked. "I thought you might have his cell phone."

"Why?"

Bobbie jumped in. "I might be moving out of town, and I wanted to talk to him about selling my home."

"Oh." Whether she believed Bobbie or not, she said, "I don't have his number."

"Okay," Bobbie said. "Well, thanks anyway."

After she closed the door behind Jenna, Bobbie said, "She's lying."

"I'll see if I can find his number online," I said. "We're running out of time."

"I'd better call Gypsy and tell her they might need to find a replacement for me for the competition," Bobbie said glumly. "I don't know who they'll be able to find on such short notice."

Bobbie and Gypsy talked for nearly half an hour, while I tried unsuccessfully to find Mr. Chen's address or a phone number other than his office number. When Bobbie hung up from her call, she slumped on the sofa.

"Let's go out to eat," I suggested, avoiding the obvious, that this might be our last day together in Arrow Springs for a long while. It didn't seem like we'd gotten any closer to finding the murderer. I remembered the state of my bank account. "Never mind. I forgot I'm broke."

"When did that ever stop you?" Bobbie gave me a half-hearted wink to let me know she was kidding. "I'll buy. Where should we go?"

"Anyplace other than the Gastro Gnome. I've only just stopped having nightmares."

"It's a gorgeous day and it's starting to warm up. Let's go to the Blue Moon Bistro in Big Springs and sit on the terrace."

I raised my eyebrows. That place was pricy. "Are you sure?"

"Unless you don't want to drive that far."

"We don't have time for a leisurely lunch. If we don't solve this murder by tomorrow—"

Bobbie reached out and rubbed my arm. "I know, dear. I just think we're too close to it. Maybe, if we get away for a couple of hours, get a change of scenery, maybe something will jiggle into place in our brains."

That sounded like as good an excuse as any. "I'll grab my jacket."

Twenty minutes later, we were seated at the edge of the restaurant's terrace overlooking Big Springs Lake. I avoided looking at the prices on the menu.

Umbrellas shielded us from the sun's glare, and propane heaters protected us from the cool air. The lake sparkled below as speed boats streaked across the water. I felt the stress of the last few days melt away, but I couldn't shake the feeling that this was a sort of last supper for Bobbie and me.

My mother would arrive tomorrow to take us back to L.A. We'd talked about how we could fight her, but even with Bobbie's money, she didn't have Angela's resources. My mother could and would fight dirty if she wanted something.

"You could skip town," I suggested.

Bobbie laughed. "I'm not on the run from the law, Whit."

"No, you're right. It would be easier to outrun the police than my mother."

Bobbie ordered a plate of bruschetta for the two of us and a glass of white wine for herself. I ordered a glass of prosecco.

"The murders seem so distant sitting here enjoying the view and the gorgeous weather," I said.

"Let's not talk about it right now. I think our minds could use a break. Maybe we'll have some more ideas when we're fresh."

The server returned with our drinks and appetizer, and we both ordered French onion soup. I didn't have much of an appetite lately, with all the worries on my mind, but the bruschetta smelled garlicky and delicious. I bit into a piece, dropping tomato chunks on my plate.

A woman approached our table. "Bobbie? Is that you?"

Bobbie squinted at the woman, a nicely put together sixty- or seventy-something wearing an outfit straight from a department store's fall catalog. Some people had no imagination. "Jilly?"

Bobbie invited her to join us, but Jilly said she was with a friend.

She hesitated. "Oh, just for a moment," she said and pulled up a chair. She proceeded to ask Bobbie about everything she'd heard from the rumor mill, starting with the murders.

"And I can't believe that developer has managed to buy up half the town without anyone realizing what he's up to. I hear he has plans for a retail complex with a Starbucks and an Olive Garden."

Bobbie and I eyed each other. "What developer?"

Jilly's eyes widened. "You haven't heard? He's planning to tear down at least twenty houses for the new complex. I heard he found a loophole in the zoning laws." She looked over her shoulder. "Looks like our food arrived. Great seeing you."

Bobbie and I stared at each other before saying in unison, "Mr. Chen."

"But he has an alibi," I said.

"From Jenna. He might have asked her to lie for him."

"What do we do now? Talk to Jenna again and get her to tell us the truth?" We'd already tried that once.

"We need to track him down."

The server put two bowls of soup in front of us, and Bobbie asked if it would be possible to get them to go. I resumed searching for an address or phone number for the developer.

"What a liar." I berated myself for believing his story without a second thought. I repeated his words in an annoying tone. "'I'm looking for a home for my mother.' What a crock."

"Even if his alibi checks out, he could have hired someone to kill Martha," Bobbie said. "There must have been a lot riding on this development."

"But I still don't understand. He can't buy Martha's or Sheila's homes now that they're dead—they won't be on the market for months until the estates are settled."

Bobbie knitted her brow in concentration. "Maybe that wasn't his motive. Maybe they found out what he was doing. If the word got out, he'd have to pay way more for the houses he bought. Or the entire community might have rallied against the development."

I nodded, although I wasn't convinced. "I suppose that's possible."

I drove us back to Arrow Springs while Bobbie called her friends, hoping to learn how to reach Mr. Chen. Her voice became more frustrated with each call.

She hung up from the last call as I pulled into her driveway. "Why couldn't we have learned about the development on a weekday when we could have gone to see him at his office? Angela will be here tomorrow—"

"Maybe," I interrupted her. "If you move to Beverly Hills, *temporarily*, I could stay here and work with Bernard. As soon as the murderer is behind bars, you can come back."

"I like the way you think, but Angela's not going to let you stay here any more than me."

She had a point. I dragged myself out of the car, heavy under the weight of the impediments standing in our way and followed Bobbie inside. "Why are we letting her tell us how to live our lives?"

Bobbie gave me a condescending smile, as if finding my naivete amusing. "Let's get back to the problem at hand, shall we? What if Mr. Chen left the office, and Jenna didn't see him go? Or maybe she's covering for him. Or he might have paid her to lie. We need to question him, but we can't wait until Monday."

"Chill out," I said. "We've got the whole interwebs at our disposal."

"Interwebs?" She gave me a quizzical look. "Is that another one of your funny words?"

"Yes. Aren't I clever?"

Chapter Twenty-Two

I retrieved my laptop from my room and set it up on the dining room table while Bobbie heated our leftovers.

After an hour of searching, I finally found Mr. Chen's address and we were back in the car. He lived on the outskirts of town, and my phone navigation led me right to his front door. His house, more modest than I'd expected, had a great location, hovering on a cliff overlooking the valley.

I knocked on the front door and we waited. A woman appeared, dark hair in a bob and wearing wool slacks and a silk shirt. The outfit gave her an affluent yet understated appearance.

"Hello." Bobbie smiled sweetly. "Mrs. Chen?"

"Yes," she said, a tentative smile on her lips. "May I help you?"

Bobbie's smile broadened. "Is Mr. Chen in?"

"He's running an errand. May I ask what this is regarding?"

Bobbie's smile turned into a frown. "Oh, dear. This is awkward."

Mrs. Chen's eyes roamed from Bobbie to me and back again. "Why don't you come in?"

We followed her into a luxuriously appointed living space with an impressive view of the valley below. "Wow," I said, walking toward the windows. "You can see the ocean from here."

Mrs. Chen smiled. "Yes, on a clear day like today. In the summer we get a great view of the smog. May I offer you something to drink?"

Before I could answer, Bobbie declined for both of us. I scowled at her, thinking a glass of water might have been nice.

Mrs. Chen motioned for us to take a seat on the sofa and sat primly in an armchair across from us. "Who is it this time?"

"Huh?" I asked. Bobbie nudged me harder than necessary. "Ouch."

"This may seem like an odd question, but do you know if your husband spent the entire day at his office on the day of the Fossil Fest?"

Her eyebrows rose slightly. "If she's claiming that my husband was with her that day, then she's lying. He spent the afternoon here, with me."

"So, he wasn't at the office with Jenna?" Bobbie asked.

Mrs. Chen tilted her head to one side. "Jenna? But Jenna isn't..." She gave an awkward chuckle and her smile returned. "This isn't about my husband's, shall we say, indiscretions, then?"

Bobbie returned her smile. "No, not at all."

"Well, that's a relief." She sighed and looked away. In a sad, soft voice, she said, "You think you'll get used to it, but you never do."

"I'm sorry," Bobbie said, her voice tender. "But Jenna claimed he was at the office with her all day through lunch and we needed to make sure."

Mrs. Chen's composure and smile had returned. "He spent the afternoon here, with me, then we went to the festival together that evening. What's this about, anyway?"

"It's not important." I gave Bobbie a nod and she stood. "Thank you so much. You've been very helpful."

On the short drive home, Bobbie stayed silent, but I had a good idea what she was thinking. Mr. Chen had an alibi, but Jenna didn't.

Bobbie sent me out to the deck to enjoy the still-warm afternoon while she made a pot of coffee. The first time I'd hung out on the deck, I'd chased Kit through the woods and found Rosa. It had been Nancy who'd put baby oil on the steps and caused Rosa's injury. Quite a coincidence that one person had set about to injure seniors in the community and another person had killed two others. It seemed like there should be a connection.

Bobbie stepped onto the deck with two mugs and set one down next to me.

"What if, after the accidents that had happened, someone got the idea of making Martha's death look like an accident?" I picked up the coffee cup and took a sip.

"Maybe," Bobbie said. "Do you think Jenna is smart

enough to come up with a plan like that?" She leaned back in her chair, looking deflated. "I'm having trouble believing Jenna is a murderer. I've known her since she was a child."

"And you never noticed she seemed unhinged?"

She shook her head. "I wouldn't say unhinged. Enthusiastic, maybe, or passionate."

"Ha! Obsessive is more like it." I took a sip of coffee while I told my mind to focus. "But let's not jump to conclusions." That had already gotten me into trouble with Ralph. "I can't help but think there must be a connection. Some women were injured and two killed."

"I see what you're getting at," Bobbie said. "So, are we back to thinking Nancy killed Martha and Sheila?"

I shook my head. "I just don't see it. She's not strong enough."

Bobbie sighed. "We're going to need to talk to Jenna again."

"Really?" In my opinion, once a day was more than enough. "I don't know what good that would do."

Bobbie persisted. "I'll call her and invite her back over."

"If Jenna killed Martha and Sheila, don't you think it would be better to meet her in a public place?" I worried that inviting Jenna over to our house meant she could come anytime she wanted, sort of like a vampire. Jenna had a lot in common with vampires, it seemed to me.

Bobbie called Jenna but got her voicemail. She left a friendly message inviting her to have dinner with us that evening.

My phone buzzed with a text from my mother. She

planned to arrive the next afternoon and told us to be ready. She didn't want to wait around all day for us.

Heaven forbid we inconvenience her while she ordered us to do her bidding.

I decided to suck it up and sent Jenna a text, telling her we'd treat her to dinner at any restaurant she chose. She answered right away.

"Ugh," I moaned when I saw her response.

"What's wrong?"

I heard the concern in Bobbie's voice, so I said, "Nothing." I stared at the text, frowning. *Can we go to the Gastro Gnome?*

I stood, facing the inevitable. I repeated my favorite affirmation. "I'm strong. I'm brave. I'm invincible." I took a deep, cleansing breath. "I can handle even this."

I wore sunglasses even though the sun had already dipped below the trees. They didn't help the visual assault. The ceramic gnomes mocked me with their cheerful smiles.

When we stepped inside, I learned the dinner hours offered additional sensory hell—polka music. As a host in a red cone hat approached, I nearly turned back to the safety of my car when Jenna saw us and waved from a booth.

"You can handle this on your own, can't you?" I said to Bobbie under my breath. "I'll just wait for you outside."

"Come on, chicken. She's harmless." She grabbed my arm. "At least as long as we're not alone with her."

"She's not what I'm afraid of," I said. "But if I go berserk in the middle of the salad course, I warned you."

Bobbie chuckled, thinking I was kidding. We slid into the booth and greeted the possibly homicidal maniac.

Jenna grinned brightly. "I just love this place, don't you?"

"You have no idea." I picked up a menu and tried to tune out the music long enough to read the offerings.

"Nice to see you again, Jenna," Bobbie said.

"Thank you so much for taking me to dinner. Have you ever had their beef stew? It's simply scrumptious."

We ordered three bowls of beef stew, and the server soon placed a basket of warm biscuits on the table. I tore one apart, slathered it with butter, and took a big bite. As the flaky goodness melted in my mouth, I decided maybe this restaurant wasn't a creation of the devil after all. When I sampled the stew, my whole outlook on the place began to change.

Bobbie waited until we'd nearly finished eating before telling Jenna why we'd asked her there. She got right to the point, but her tone was gentle. "I understand you may not have been entirely truthful."

Jenna's happy face froze. "What do you mean?" The muscles holding her smile in place began to slacken as her eyes darted from Bobbie to me.

It was up to me to play bad cop again. "You told me you and Mr. Chen were at the office the entire day of the Fossil Fest. But Mr. Chen was at home with his wife all afternoon. You lied."

She blinked rapidly and swallowed. "I guess I forgot."

"No, you didn't," I said impatiently. I really hated when people lied to me. "Where were you that afternoon?"

She cast her eyes downward. "Please don't tell Mr. Chen." She looked up, a glimmer of hope in her eyes. "I wanted a new outfit to wear to the Fossil Fest, so I went shopping. I knew Luke was going to be there. I had all my work done." She pouted. "Mr. Chen never lets me have time off."

"Where'd you go shopping?" I asked.

"The mall at Big Springs."

I turned to Bobbie. "There's a mall in Big Springs?"

She chuckled. "If you want to call a dozen stores and a food court a mall, then yes."

Turning my attention back to Jenna, I asked, "Can you prove where you were?"

Her eyes widened. "Prove? Why do I need to prove...?" She gasped as the realization hit her. "You don't think I killed Martha?"

Conversations around us quieted, and I felt dozens of eyes watching us. I spoke quietly so the other diners wouldn't hear me. "Keep your voice down, please. Can you prove where you were or not? Do you have a receipt from something you bought?"

Her eyes began to well up with tears. "I couldn't find anything I liked. I bought a corn dog, but I didn't keep the receipt." She began to sob.

Bobbie nudged me. "Back off," she said under her breath.

My jaw clenched as my temper rose. Were we going to let a few tears get in the way of finding out the truth? "Fine. I'll wait for you in the car."

I slid out of the booth and stomped my way out of the restaurant. Once outside, I took a deep breath of crisp mountain air and paced the parking lot until Bobbie emerged.

"Why did you go soft on her?" I asked. "She might be a murderer."

"Have you never heard you catch more flies with honey?" After my blank look, she added, "I got the names of the shops she visited."

"Who's going to remember a brown-haired, average height woman from several days ago?"

Bobbie held up her phone. "I have her picture."

"Okay, fine. Let's go to the mall then." I was still convinced that it would likely be a futile trip.

"To the mall."

When Bobbie and I emerged from the imaginatively named Big Springs Mall, I grumbled, "You'd think someone would have remembered someone as perky as Jenna. That was a total waste of time."

She took a bite of her soft pretzel. "Not at all, dear."

"I'm really happy you found the patchouli oil you've been looking for, and you seem to be enjoying your pretzel, but we're no closer to solving the murder."

"Au contraire. We finally have a suspect without an alibi. All we have to do now is prove Jenna killed Martha and Sheila." She frowned. "I have to admit, I didn't think she had it in her. I mean, I've known for years she was a little unbalanced, but I never expected this."

On the drive home, we discussed how to prove Jenna's involvement.

"Fingerprints?" I suggested. "DNA?"

Bobbie shook her head. "Jenna admitted being in Martha's house. If there are fingerprints in Sheila's house, she'd just say she'd been there too. It doesn't prove anything."

"What about fingerprints in Martha's basement? If Jenna's are there, I'd like to see her give a credible reason for that."

Bobbie considered this idea. "Let's stop by at Arrow Investigations on the way home."

"It's Saturday. Remember? Not to mention a holiday weekend."

"Fine," she grumbled. "Give me your phone and I'll call him."

Bobbie and Bernard had a long conversation that didn't sound promising from what I could hear. She relayed the highlights. "Since the police consider Martha's death an accident, they didn't check for fingerprints. Mr. Fernsby said he'll see if he can convince them to dust the basement, but it's not going to happen for at least a few days."

When we got home, Bobbie put on another pot of coffee, and I began to wonder if I'd ever sleep again. We took our spots around the dining room table with notebooks and pens at hand. Our brainstorming, while energetic at first, began to veer off into more and more imaginative and implausible tangents. At midnight, we had to admit that we'd run out of time, ideas, and suspects.

She stood and carried her cup to the kitchen. "I give up. But I'm not about to go stay with your mother. The Beverly Hills lifestyle doesn't agree with me. What am I supposed to do all day in that town? I bet she wouldn't even let me touch the garden—I might ruin the symmetry. Blah. I hate symmetry."

I happened to be a fan of symmetry and all things orderly, but she was right. She didn't belong there, and I didn't think she'd last two weeks with my mother.

"In the morning, we'll figure something out." I used the most reassuring voice I could muster.

"And I'll have to let the other Ukulele Ladies know," she said glumly. "It's just two weeks until the competition. I might be able to make it back for the Winter Fest but we need a lot more rehearsal. We've lost our focus with everything that's been going on."

"I'll make some calls in the morning. With your money and my connections, we should be able to find someplace else to stay."

"Not too far away," Bobbie suggested. "We still have a murderer to catch."

Chapter Twenty-Three

At six a.m. the phone buzzed, and I squinted at the bedside clock. Who would be texting me at this time of the morning?

The text was from Luke. *Up for a run?*

I wanted to find out what he knew about Jenna and her possible involvement in the murders, so I replied. *Sure. Meet you at the bear 6:30.*

The moment I saw him, I flashed back to the first and only time I'd met him for a run, the day after we found Martha's body. The image of pink, fuzzy slippers popped into my mind unbidden, and I felt a rush of anger toward the killer. A run would help take care of that. Finding out who killed Martha and why they did it would be even better.

"Hey." He held out his hand and we fist bumped, then headed toward the river.

"I remember the first time we went for a run. You told

me not to go that direction." I pointed in the opposite direction where the rockslide blocked the road.

Yeah." He kept his gaze forward, his expression unreadable.

"That's where Kit found Sheila, did you know that?"

He nodded and mumbled something I couldn't hear.

"What was that?"

"Let's run." He took off and I followed.

I easily kept up with him as he followed the river, but when we came to a small bridge, he crossed it to the other side. We hadn't gone that way on our last run.

"Hey," I called at his back as he sped up. Breathing heavily, I tried keeping up, but he was in even better shape than me. I'd have to consider cutting back on the cinnamon rolls.

The path led to a fire road that cut into the mountain. It sloped slowly upward, and I began to get frustrated. Where was he taking me?

He finally slowed to a jog, then stopped. Looking off the side of the cliff, I saw the river flowing lazily below us.

"What's going on, Whit?" he asked. "Why are you asking so many questions?"

Feigning an innocent expression, I asked, "What are you talking about?"

"Don't play games with me. I know you're helping Bobbie investigate the murders. You should just leave it up to the police."

"I know about you and Sheila." I wasn't sure why I said it, but I wanted to see his reaction.

His lips tightened into a sneer. "What? What do you think you know?"

"I know she gave you thousands of dollars. What did she want in return?"

He turned away, and I wasn't sure he would answer. "It was a loan to upgrade my studio. No big deal. She told me I could pay it back later when my career took off."

"But she wanted something in return, didn't she?"

He walked further up the road, and I stayed close behind. I pulled my phone out of my pocket, doing my best to be discreet, but when he turned back around, I held it behind my back.

"Give me that, and I'll tell you what happened." He reached for the phone. When I didn't comply, he repeated his demand and stepped closer. "Give me the phone."

I held it out tentatively, and before I could react, he grabbed it and hurled it off the side of the cliff.

"What did you do that for?" I asked.

"I don't want us to be interrupted before I can explain."

"Go ahead." I willed my voice to sound calm while every cell of my body signaled danger. "Explain."

"I know what you think, but I'm not a murderer."

"Maybe not. But you did kill her."

"I didn't mean to," he said. "It was an accident. Sheila invested in my recording studio, but then she wanted more than a business relationship. She started telling me what to do and where to go. If I even talked to another girl, she'd get crazy jealous."

"You could have given her back the money," I said.

"I'd already spent it on recording equipment. But even if I had given her the money back, I don't think she would have let me walk away. When I told her I wanted out, she freaked. She came at me, hitting and kicking me like a madwoman. I pushed her away and she fell and hit her head."

My heart pounded while I did my best to appear calm. "So, it was an accident. Nobody goes to jail for an accident." I waited for a response, but he silently hung his head, the picture of remorse. "Why didn't you call the paramedics?"

He took a few steps toward a pile of fallen tree limbs. He sat on a thick log and put his face into his hands. "She was already dead. What was the point?"

"And your problem was solved. You no longer had to pay back the money."

He looked up and looked me in the eye. "They would have charged me with murder. The money I owed her meant I had a motive. I couldn't take that chance."

"And you wouldn't have been able to cash the second check if she was dead." I waited for him to respond, but he didn't. "Was Martha a problem too?"

His cold eyes gave me a chill. "She was waiting for me when I got home—wanted to know why I was so filthy. I made excuses, but when she heard Sheila left town suddenly, she put two and two together. She wanted me to go to the police and tell them what happened. If I didn't, she said she would. I couldn't let her do that." He reached out and wrapped his hand around a fallen branch the size of a club and stood.

I took a step back as he approached me. I could turn and run, but he'd overtake me in no time. I had plenty of endurance, but he was the faster runner.

Time slowed the way it did when I was in the zone

and I braced myself, centered and ready for his attack. He swung the heavy branch at me, and I barely avoided the makeshift weapon as it scraped against my chest.

"Are you planning to kill me, too?" I asked, sounding braver than I felt.

"What choice do I have, Whit?"

More prepared for the next shot, I ducked under the club and propelled myself toward his knees, hoping to knock him off balance.

He fell on his back but jumped to his feet before I did. I stayed in a crouch, waiting for his next move and deciding on mine. We were too close to the edge of the cliff for comfort, and as much as I didn't want either of us going down the side, better him than me.

Springing forward, I pushed one of his legs out from under him. He cried out as he fell but he managed to grab my ankle. As I yanked it away from him, he knocked me off balance and I fell on top of him.

He flipped me on my back and lay on top of me with my wrists pinned to the ground. In a different situation, it would have been a turn-on.

He gave me a sly smile. "You like it rough, huh?"

I bit his arm. Hard.

He cried out and slapped me across the face, which hurt, but gave me a chance to break free. As I scrambled to my feet, he grabbed the branch from the ground, holding it horizontally in front of him. If I took a step back, I'd go over the cliff and down to the river.

Breathing heavily, I waited to see what he would do. I didn't have to wait long. He took a step toward me, then shoved the branch and his body against me full force.

There was no time to think as I lost footing, but I didn't need to think. I had spent my entire adult life falling off things. As if in slow motion, I rolled down the side of the cliff until I could grab hold of a tree root.

I focused on my surroundings. The nearly vertical drop sloped slightly, with tree roots and boulders jutting out from the loose dirt and pebbles. As I planned my descent, the root began to give way.

I found a foothold for my left foot and leaned against the cliffside, my face pressed into dirt, pebbles, and clumps of near-dead vegetation. I craned my head to look up, but there was no way to climb back to the road. The only way was down.

Luke knew that. He'd be waiting for me at the bottom unless I could get there before him.

Luckily, I'd learned to rock climb when I'd had a crush on a guy who taught at the gym. When his boyfriend stopped by to pick him up one day, I quit. I'd have to stop by and thank him, assuming I survived.

Slowly, I inched my way down, one careful step at a time, but the progress was painfully slow. After what felt like half an hour, I lost footing and slid for a few feet, a boulder stopping my descent. That would leave a bruise, but it would have good company with all the other scrapes and bruises.

The slope became less vertical, and I sat on a rock about ten feet from the bottom, surveying the river and surrounding area. There was no sign of Luke along the river. I couldn't be that lucky, could I?

My heart pounded in my chest. With the hem of my shirt, I wiped sweat from my forehead, leaving a muddy streak behind. I had every reason to panic, but that would only make matters worse. "One step at a time, Whit," I whispered. More like one scooch at a time, as I scooted on my behind toward the river.

I froze and tuned into the sounds around me, sensing danger. Scanning the trees below, I imagined Luke lurking behind one waiting for me. I'd have to make a run for it—what choice did I have?

As soon as the ground leveled enough for me to stand, I scoured the landscape for an escape route. Walking toward the river, I screamed when Luke dropped out of a nearby tree. I took off in the opposite direction. Rocks and sticks lay hidden under a carpet of pine needles, and if I fell or twisted an ankle, that might be the end of me. I'd have to take that chance.

Footsteps crunching behind me pushed me to go faster and I imagined the feel of his breath on my neck. With a sinking feeling, I realized I couldn't outrun him.

The trees on either side of the river were gnarled with branches. Climbing one wouldn't do me any good—it would just make me a sitting duck. I ran for a tree with a sturdy-looking limb, hoping I judged the height correctly. With Luke close behind, I veered toward it and jumped for the branch. Grabbing hold of it, I swung my legs high just like I did on the uneven bars, then spun around and kicked him hard in the chest.

I didn't stick around to see how long he'd stay down.

Chapter Twenty-Four

With my heart pounding in my ears, I took off at full speed along the dirt path on the other side of the river, desperately hoping it led to the road. When I hit pavement, I slowed slightly, looking for signs of life—someone out for an early walk or a drive who could save me before Luke caught up with me.

At the sound of a car, I slowed and waved my arms. When it drove past, I shouted after it, using some language that Bobbie wouldn't have approved of. I kept running, my lungs ready to burst but adrenaline pushing me on.

The next car that came by slowed down, and I did my best to not look like a maniac. Considering I was covered in dirt and sweat, that wasn't an easy task. I felt hope rise when the car pulled over and hurried to the passenger door as the window rolled down.

My hope faded at the sight of Jenna's ponytail.

"Get in," she called to me.

"No way." I backed away from the car looking for

something to dive behind if she decided to run me down with her Ford. After everything I'd been through already, I wasn't going to let a perky psycho-stalker take me down.

"He's coming," she yelled, easing the car forward to follow me.

A quick look over my shoulder told me she was right. I'd normally be impressed at Luke's endurance, but now it just pissed me off. I took off again, and Jenna's car pulled ahead of me, squealing to a stop. She threw open her door and jumped out, facing me with a determined scowl.

I ran into the middle of the street to get away from her, but she didn't chase me. Instead, she turned to face Luke as he approached.

He came to a stop in front of her, panting heavily. "Jenna." He struggled to catch his breath. "What are you doing here?"

"I'm here to stop you."

"Stupid girl." Luke bent over, and for a moment I thought he was crying. When he straightened up, I realized it was laughter. "You think—" Out of breath, he didn't finish the sentence.

"Yes, Luke. I think I'm going to stop you from killing anyone else."

"But baby." He'd stopped laughing now, and spoke seductively, a technique that must have worked on her plenty of times before. "If I go to jail, so will you."

Her eyes widened. "No, I won't. Why would I?"

"Because you helped me. You helped me carry Sheila. Don't you remember?"

"You said she went out of town," Jenna began, her voice trembling. "You said you had to get rid of her carpet because you'd ruined it. You said she'd be mad. You said you were going to buy her another one and she'd never know the difference."

"Do you think anyone will believe you?" Luke asked, his voice mocking. "Do you think anyone will believe that you didn't know what I was doing at Martha's house?"

I came closer and stood behind Jenna. "Jenna's not going to jail—I'll make sure of it." At least I'd do my best. "But you are. For a long, long time." I tapped Jenna on the shoulder. "Get in the car and let's get out of here."

Jenna hesitated. "But—"

"Get in the car!"

Jenna did as ordered. At the sound of the engine starting, I crept backward keeping an eye on Luke. Then I heard the barking. *Not now.*

Sure enough, Kit appeared and ran over to me, barking and yipping, and then to Luke, prancing happily in front of him. Luke took advantage of the distraction to lunge at me, his hands aiming for my throat. I pulled back and grabbed him by his wrists, holding on with all the strength I had left.

"Hey!" he cried as he wrenched his arms from my grasp. Kit had taken hold of his ankle. He shook his leg to get her off. "Let go, you little runt." He swung his leg hard, and Kit went flying off the side of the road.

Anger gave me the extra push I needed. I leaped into the air as if gravity had no effect on me, twisting, and kicking the way I'd practiced so many times. My foot connected with Luke's head.

He went down and I rushed to Kit's side, scooped her up, and jumped into the passenger seat.

Kit gave my chin a lick and I held her tight.

◆ ⟶ ⟶

When Luke regained consciousness, he didn't wait around for the police to arrive, but it didn't take long for them to track him down. Jenna drove me home, where we found Bobbie waiting on the front lawn. She squealed at the sight of me.

I refused to go to the emergency room. All I wanted was a hot bath and a stiff drink. I didn't care that it was breakfast time, though I wouldn't say no to a big plate of bacon and eggs.

"Good idea," Bobbie said. "Get cleaned up before your parents arrive."

I groaned. I'd forgotten they'd be arriving soon. "At least now that the murderer has been caught, Angela will have to let us stay."

"She will," Bobbie said. "But if not, I've finally come up with a plan B."

"What's that?" I asked. "Laxative in the brownies?"

She chuckled. "No, but I like the way you think."

Chapter Twenty-Five

Decem ber rolled around, along with the Winter Festival and Craft Fair. With Kit curled up in my lap, and me bundled up in my warmest jacket, we waited for the Ukulele Ladies, the last musicians of the day, to be announced. An outdoor stage had been set up for the competition, and I'd just endured a barbershop quartet that gave new meaning to singing off key. Kiss My Brass sounded flat without Luke and his French horn, or perhaps they were feeling down after finding out one of their members was a murderer.

Elijah appeared, holding two cups of hot apple cider. He pointed to my lighted headband. "Nice antlers. Mind if I join you?"

I patted the seat on my right. "Anyone who comes bearing food or drink is welcome."

A gruff voice behind me said, "Good thing I brought cinnamon rolls."

I turned to see Bernard Fernsby, rumpled as ever, with

a bakery box. I scooted down to make room for him on my left.

Grinning, I opened the box and inhaled the delicious scent.

"What did I miss?" Bernard asked as I took a roll and several napkins and handed him back the box.

"Just about everyone," I said. "My money's on the Blarney Band. Luke was right. They're really good."

"Speaking of Luke," Elijah said, "sorry your friend turned out to be a murderer."

I shrugged, not wanting to go into my feelings of betrayal. "Oh, you know. Win some, lose some."

"How did you figure out he'd murdered those women?" Elijah asked.

"I guess I'm a natural sleuth." I left out the part about confronting him at the worst possible time, leading to him confessing and trying to kill me.

Bernard shook his head. "Why did Jenna lie for him?"

"She would have done anything for him," I said. "And he'd told her so many lies, I'm not sure she knew what the truth was anymore."

"Here's what I don't understand," Elijah said. "If Sheila's death was an accident, why not call an ambulance or the cops? Why bury her?"

"Luke claims he didn't think he'd be believed since he owed Sheila all that money," I said. "And then there was the last check she gave him the day she died. Four thousand dollars. He needed time to cash it."

The emcee came to the microphone and announced the next act: The Ukulele Ladies.

We stood to clap and cheer as Bobbie and the rest of

the group took the stage. The crowd shouted louder than it had for any of the other groups, maybe partly because word had spread about Bobbie and me catching a murderer.

Bobbie came up to the microphone while Rosa, Gypsy, and Ralph took their seats, and the crowd hushed.

I leaned over to Bernard. "Wait until you hear them play Bohemian Rhapsody. It's quite impressive."

Elijah chuckled. "I've been hearing Gypsy practicing the high notes for weeks."

A woman in the row in front of us turned around and shushed us as Bobbie began to speak.

"This song is dedicated to someone very special to me. She's a hero, and the whole town should be very proud of her."

I did my best to appear humble as she sat down, and the quartet began to play. The moment I recognized the song, I jumped to my feet with Kit squirming in my arms.

Elijah tugged at my sleeve. "Sit down," he whispered.

"You Ain't Nothin' but a Hound Dog?" Feeling everyone's eyes on me, I sat back down. Once again, that darned dog had stolen my thunder.

Bobbie caught my eye in the crowd and gave me a wink.

They followed up the Elvis song with Bohemian Rhapsody, and the crowd roared with approval. After the four "Ladies" took their bows, Bobbie joined us in the audience, Jenna trailing along behind her, pushing a stroller. She'd made a deal with the prosecutor to testify against Luke. She'd be on probation for a long, long time, but I was glad she wouldn't be spending time in jail.

"Babysitting?" I asked.

Jenna pulled back a blanket, revealing Mr. Whiskers in a festive holiday sweater and bonnet. I tried but failed to keep from snickering. *Poor thing.* My opinion changed when I heard the unmistakable sound of purring.

"Thank you so much for letting me keep Mr. Whiskers," Jenna said. "He's the best friend I've ever had." After a brief pause, she added shyly, "Next to you, Whit. And you, Bobbie."

"Kit is forever grateful," I said in my usual sarcastic tone. Bobbie elbowed me. "I'm so glad you could give Mr. Whiskers a home. I can see, or I should say *hear*, he's very happy."

Bobbie gave Jenna a hug and sat down next to Bernard. "Shush, everyone. They're about to announce the winners."

When the votes came in, the Blarney Band had won, as expected, but the Ukulele Ladies came in second place. The Soul Sisters scowled as they accepted their trophy, obviously disappointed to come in third place.

When Bobbie returned with her trophy, she wiped away a tear.

"I'm sorry you didn't win, Bobbie," I said.

"Are you kidding? I'm thrilled we came in second. I just wish Martha could be here to share in the day. She loved performing."

Bernard stood and said his goodbyes, adding to Bobbie, "See you in the office Monday morning."

As soon as he left, I huffed, "You're still going to work with Bernard after everything that happened?" Like me nearly being killed, I wanted to add.

"Of course," Bobbie said. "The publicity after we solved Sheila and Martha's murders will get us lots of new clients for our business."

"Our business?" I hoped she didn't include me in her plans.

"Mr. Fernsby has agreed to take me on as a partner. My investment will allow us to advertise and drum up more clients. Eventually, after I have my license, he plans to retire. I figured you could help. You could use some money until you move back to Los Angeles, couldn't you? You have a knack for investigating, you know."

"Seems to me I have a knack for accusing the wrong people of murder and finding out who's sleeping with whom."

"That might come in handy." Bobbie took my arm as we walked to the car. "I've always wanted a sidekick."

"I've always wanted world peace and low-calorie baked goods that don't taste like cardboard. You can't always get what you want, as The Stones said."

"I know, I know. You get what you need." Bobbie grinned. "But sometimes, when you least expect it, what you want and what you need are exactly the same thing."

My phone rang and the display showed the caller as Arrow Springs Veterinary Clinic.

"Ms. Leland?" a woman asked.

"That's me. But please call me Whit."

"Ms. Leland, this is Arrow Springs Veterinary Clinic. We've had confirmation on Kit's microchips. The first is registered to Mrs. Angela Leland. I believe that's your mother?"

"Yes," I said. "And the second?"

"The second is registered to a Mr. Jonathan Vance."

"Were you able to find out why he gave up his dog?"

"That's the problem, Ms. Leland," she said. "He didn't relinquish his pet. In fact, he reported her stolen."

The noise of the crowd faded to a dull roar, and my voice caught in my throat. I managed to get one word out: "Stolen?"

Bobbie hurried over to my side. "What is it, Whit? What's been stolen?"

I held up my index finger, not wanting to miss the woman's reply.

"I'll have to notify the police and give them your information," she said.

"I see." I disconnected from the call and tried to focus on Bobbie's anxious face.

"They're going to take Kit away from us." Tears threatened to erupt as I buried my face in Kit's fur.

Bobbie crossed her arms, her voice strong and defiant. "Not if I have anything to say about it." She scanned the crowd. "Mr. Fernsby!" she called out, waving him over. "We have our next case!"

Thank you for reading *Old Fashioned Murder, an Arrow Investigations Humorous, Action-Adventure Mystery!*

To learn about Arrow Investigations next case involving Kit's former owner, look for *Hair of the Dog*—coming in early 2023.

If you haven't yet read the Arrow Investigations prequel, *The Black Daiquiri*, you can download it when you sign up for updates at www.kcwalker.com.

❦ ❦

KC Walker also writes and publishes sweet cozy mysteries under the name Karen Sue Walker. You can find her Bridal Shop Mysteries on most sales platforms and Haunted Tearoom Mysteries on Amazon. Visit karensuewalker.com to learn more.

By the way, I love hearing from readers—you can email me at kc@karensuewalker.com.

Ingram Content Group UK Ltd.
Milton Keynes UK
UKHW012254080523
421436UK00019B/431/J